SO, WHAT KEPT YOU?

SO, WHAT KEPT YOU?

New stories inspired by
Anton Chekhov and Raymond Carver

Edited by Claire Malcolm
and Margaret Wilkinson

Foreword by Tess Gallagher

FlambardPress

new
writing
north

First published in Great Britain in 2006 by Flambard Press
Stable Cottage, East Fourstones, Hexham NE47 5DX
www.flambardpress.co.uk

In association with New Writing North
2 School Lane, Whickham, Newcastle upon Tyne NE16 4SL
www.newwritingnorth.com

Typeset by BookType
Cover Design by Gainford Design Associates
Front cover image: 'Urban Window' by Anja Percival,
reproduced by kind permission
Printed in Great Britain by Cromwell Press, Trowbridge, Wiltshire

A CIP catalogue record for this book is available from the British Library.
ISBN-13: 9781873226841
ISBN-10: 1873226845

'Trachtenbauer' by Ali Smith was first published in
Ali Smith's Supersonic 70s (Penguin, 2005)

Flambard Press wishes to thank Arts Council England for its financial support.

Flambard Press is a member of Inpress
and of Independent Northern Publishers.

Contents

Unselfing

'A writer must unself himself . . .' (V.S. Pritchett, writing of Chekhov)

Perhaps one of a writer's favourite ways of unseating the self is to hitch a ride on something partial from another writer who inspires us. We can purloin a scrap, a line and a phrase, an image – something that on its face is even drab and unremarkable – but if it works its alchemy in us, we can use it to open the imagination freshly.

The pretext of Margaret Wilkinson's generative idea for this book greatly appealed to me, combining as it does the impetus of two short-story masters, Anton Chekhov and my late husband, Raymond Carver, in whose company contemporary writers might draw forth their own stories.

Both Ray and Chekhov seem ideal candidates for extending an invitation to cadge, to piggy-back, or take a leg-up from their shards and flickers, for they both seemed to feel that it mattered not a wit who did the great writing, only that it get done. They also made a point of submerging their own personal mandates in order to throw into better relief the plights of their characters. Chekhov wrote: 'When you want to touch the reader's heart, try to be colder. It gives their grief, as it were, a background against which it stands out in greater relief.'

It wasn't easy for Ray to be 'colder'. He was, in his daily

life, a man who embraced, both in fact and metaphorically. An abiding tenderness of presence comes to mind when I think of him. But in his writing self, in his 'unselfing' into fiction, he was otherwise – not that he denied his more passionate nature, rather he put the natures of his characters first. Like Chekhov he also left some essential matters to his readers. This was, in Chekhov's time and even in Ray's, a bit revolutionary and not a little irksome to reviewers and to the laziest of their readers. When critics would have liked him to work out his endings so all had been satisfied, Ray would often walk away, leaving readers with things to resolve on their own. He had a great respect for the reader's ability to participate in the unknowns of his story and bring it to a benefit he could not have entirely designed.

In this regard I recall the heated discussions on the set of Robert Altman's *Short Cuts* about Ray's story 'So Much Water So Close to Home', which, to the point of this book, was stimulated by a news clipping. The actors and technical crew argued about whether they would have kept fishing had they discovered a woman's body in the river. The women said one thing, the men another – some men siding with the women. This oscillation was made possible because both Ray and Altman took different paths to exploring the generative incident. Altman favored letting the male character defend himself in such a way that his point of view took on more weight. Ray told the story through a woman's point of view and this skewed the story in her direction. But each of them left the question of what should have been done with the body open enough that the opposite view would come into play.

Perhaps because Chekhov and Carver were adept at

deadpanning, they also wrote with wonderful humour. In a course I taught once using Ray's stories, the class would come most alive when I had them read passages aloud, making it obvious what was hilarious. Both Chekhov and Carver have had a multitude of imitators because they make a story so transparent it seems to speak itself without benefit of even the writer. It looks easy to write such stories, but those who have tried to write in a Chekhovian or Carveresque manner will attest to the superficiality of that impression. Ray wrote as many as thirty drafts trying to get every phrase, every sentence and nuance, to hum. I know because I went over those drafts with him. Chekhov also practised a rigorous exactness. This acute attention to detail was a part of their unselfing, their taking on the mantle of coldness which paradoxically ignites fellow-feeling and, beyond that, causes us to do more than judge others. We enact their dilemmas. We inhabit their pains.

I have described elsewhere how Ray and I took passages from Chekhov for Ray's last book, *A New Path to the Waterfall*, and arranged them into lines of poetry. Chekhov was our collaborative soul mate in those final days of Ray's life. We leaned on his prose until it yielded another light and joined the new context of Ray's last poems, allowing him resonances he would not have come to without Chekhov.

I recall Ray reading aloud to me something from Tolstoy where he audaciously confesses: 'I love Chekhov!' Ray shared that love and enjoyed the fact that Tolstoy could say so without embarrassment. Ray connected with Chekhov's struggle to write in a cramped household in which the father raged at and gave beatings to his children. Chekhov would fail to save one of his brothers from alcoholism. Like Ray, he would feel his own body giving way to a consuming disease; in Chekhov's case, tuberculosis, in Ray's, lung cancer. The press of family and communal obligations would become daunting for both writers.

A photo of Chekhov in heavy coat with his dog hangs yet near the desk Ray used here in Pt Angeles. Wherever we went, that photo went with us. The two writers gazed out at each other – one looking towards what he could not guess: an American writer a world and generations away, who aspired to his example and who, in his own way, had managed more than homage. Ray had applied Chekhovian methods of concision to 1980s American life. This had yielded the-world-according-to-Carver, for neither writer would be subsumed by his influences.

Because Ray loved Chekhov, I too began to appreciate him anew. We reread him together, took up his letters, a biography or two, and determined to travel to Russia to see Chekhov's home in Yalta, his grave in Moscow. But Ray was already succumbing to the lung cancer that would claim him. To bring Chekhov close in those last days I would read a story by him in the early morning, then retell it to Ray at breakfast. By the afternoon Ray would reread the story himself. In the evening we could remark on it together. Thinking about that time now, I feel an immense gratitude that such kinships, such deep and abiding affinities, can reach across time, distance and language to companion us, both as readers and writers. It is one of the lucky miracles.

With Ray's work and Chekhov's there is an authentic sense that one may start anywhere, with any small detail or observation and that this may lead to discoveries that could illuminate the muted pains and joys we live by. The underpinning of that simple faith has become a stimulus for many different kinds of writers, young and old.

Ray was always scribbling lines and phrases on napkins and the backs of envelopes, snippets he'd overheard or read or witnessed. Sometimes I would be delegated to take down the fleeting morsel, to make sure it didn't escape into the oceanic surges of our daily life. This occasioned my giving Ray what we called his 'bathrobe notebooks', for the small spiral-hinged tablets waited in his robe pockets at the ready. When he saw there wouldn't be time for individual use of these tidbits, Ray strung together a list of the observations and quotes to make a poem. Given time enough, he could have taken any one of them as a pretext for an entire story or a poem.

There were six such notebooks with hasty penciled jottings in his nearly illegible scrawl. Like driftwood, he would have taken up each of these verbal shapes and seen something different. It was the promise of these savings that intrigued him.

Still, Ray believed one should only save things in order to use them up. He hadn't the least nostalgia for things that didn't work or yield a dividend. If a pen didn't work, he threw it into the fire. I believe he would have been glad for any writer who could bring fresh import to something he'd left behind. He would be doubly glad to be paired here with Chekhov in such a celebratory bonanza, shouldering along with writers he'd never met but who were taking hold where they could.

If he were beside me now I would read aloud to him from a letter about Chekhov's trip in a carriage to Poltava: 'What weddings we met on the road, what lovely music we heard in

11

the evening stillness, and what a heavy smell of fresh hay there was!' We would smile at each other. Ray would begin to scribble in his notebook, maybe only the words 'the heavy smell of fresh hay'.

Tess Gallagher
Sky House, 22 October 2005

Introduction

In 2002 New Writing North began what was to become a UK-wide campaign to revive the short story as a form of interest for both readers and writers. From a modest beginning in Newcastle the campaign to Save Our Stories spread, and many projects and initiatives have followed.

The writer who originally planted the idea in our heads that the short story might need some attention was Margaret Wilkinson, a New Yorker by birth who resides in the North East. At the time I was working with Margaret on the development of a new play she was writing inspired by the creative synergy that had existed between two of her favourite short-story authors, Anton Chekhov and Raymond Carver. As we developed the play – which was eventually commissioned by Northern Stage – and Margaret undertook extensive research in Russia and visited the US to meet with Tess Gallagher, our plans to stage a festival of stories around the production of the play grew.

Via the research for the play, which was eventually titled *Kaput!*, Margaret and I had come upon a book full of jottings from Chekhov's notebooks. Inspired by pages and pages of wonderful observations and fragments of ideas we decided that it would be fun to echo Carver's interest in Chekhov's life and work and commission contemporary writers to respond to a list of our favourite 'starting points' taken from notes made by both Chekhov and Carver. We decided to approach our favourite short-story writers from both the UK and the US, and to research possible contributors and make contact with writers from Eastern Europe. The resulting commissions are all included here; many of them were premiered at the Festival of Stories, which ran in Newcastle upon Tyne during October 2004.

We hope that the book will encourage readers to go back to the stories of both Chekhov and Carver and maybe even have a go at writing their own stories based on the 'starting points' that we offered to our contributors.

Claire Malcolm
Director, New Writing North

Dear Writer

Finish a story begun by Anton Chekhov. The great short-story writer left notebooks full of ideas, character names, situations, incidents and brief descriptions. As a writer who loves short stories and practices the form, use your voice to develop a fragment found among Chekhov's papers. Select from a long-list that is sure to contain something to excite your imagination. If not Chekhov, Raymond Carver. A second list contains ideas for stories Carver, often called the American Chekhov, left in his notebooks for future development. We are celebrating the short story by focusing on two writers who loved the medium – writers' writers whose work has probably already inspired many of us. We are calling for contemporary voices to re-inhabit Chekhovian and Carverian territory through finding individual, even idiosyncratic, connection to the fragments they have left. It's like a gift from these masters; a letter unopened; a dream to be interpreted; or a strange note in someone else's hand that turns up in your own pocket.

Best wishes,
Margaret Wilkinson

Starting Points for the Commissions

Anton Chekhov – from his notebooks

- Rosalie Ossipovna-Aromat.
- In a love letter: Stamp enclosed for reply.
- It was such a romantic wedding, and later – what fools! what babies!
- The parlour maid, Nadya, fell in love with an exterminator of bugs and black beetles.
- Instead of sheets, dirty tablecloths.
- A tiny little schoolboy with the name of Trachtenbauer.
- They teased the girl with castor oil, and therefore she did not marry.
- Every day after dinner the husband threatens the wife that he will become a monk, and the wife cries.
- When I married, I became an old woman.

Raymond Carver – from his notebooks

- The time I broke a tooth on barbecued ribs. I was drunk. We were all drunk.
- The early sixteenth-century Belgian painter called, for want of his real name, The Master of the Embroidered Leaf.
- Those dead birds on the porch when I opened up the house after being away for three months.
- The policeman whose nails were bitten to the quick.
- . . . just as we sit down the phone rings and is passed around the table so everyone can say something.
- Three men and a woman in wet suits. The door to their motel room is open and they are watching TV.
- Don't forget when the phone was off the hook all day, every day.
- Aunt Lola the shoplifter rolled her own dad and other drunks as well.
- I've got how much longer?

J. Robert Lennon

When I married, I became an old woman . . .

When I married, I became an old woman, and my wife became an old man. The change came upon us in the night, while we slept, in the tiny hotel in the mountains we had chosen for our honeymoon, and when we woke, the light of morning spilling across the bed, we regarded one another with compassionate unsurprise, and clasped hands as we had on that romantic night, six months before, when we first kissed on the winding path beside the river.

Our return home was greeted with earnest congratulations, delivered by our friends, neighbours, and family in deferential tones, and we assumed the duties of husband and wife as any couple might, making the necessary allowances and compromises with respectful affection and enthusiasm. For some weeks my wife tried to wear my clothes before admitting at last that she hadn't much enthusiasm for suits and ties; though she had enjoyed seeing me dressed in them, her own taste ran more toward the rumpled and rugged, and she soon could be seen doddering about the house in jeans, Oxford shirts, and tweed jackets. The sight of her chambray-clad shoulders, still broad and strong as mine had been before we married, working at a crust of fried egg stuck to the pan, filled me with a sense of contentment and well-being I hadn't known since I was a child. And while I was certainly comfortable in the cotton skirts and drooping cardigans my wife had once favored, I felt much more at home in the crisp linen suits and woolen dresses I bought to wear to work. A discomfiting looseness I felt at the office was quickly remedied by a brassiere, and though its straps chafed my bent, narrow back, it also made me feel secure and organised, as any working woman would want. Make-up, which initially I eschewed, came to seem indispensible, a strategic bit of artifice to match the stern angularity that had once been at my command when I was young, and a man. My wife had never much liked wearing make-up, or a bra for that matter, but it was she, white stubble poking through her still-handsome face, who taught me how to apply it.

My colleagues at the office seemed uncomfortable at first joking around with an old woman, but soon paper aeroplanes began to drift, as they once had, into my cubicle, and hilarious internet links found their way into my inbox. Though arthritis had slowed my typing, my mind was still sharp, and I held my own in my work and friendships. I joined in the fun at happy hour, though I was forced to refuse the foaming pints my favorite bartender still drew for me the moment I walked through the door; my body was smaller now, my appetite diminished, and I trained him to serve me a sherry instead.

Weekends I spent with my wife, at home or out doing our favourite things. Though bowling no longer satisfied, I still enjoyed our drives in the country. Initially I felt dwarfed by our car, and had to readjust the seat and mirrors into new positions, but I better appreciated its capacity to erase my fragility, to extend my physical influence. I drove more slowly than before, allowing for my more sluggish reflexes, my fading vision. My wife sat sprawled in the passenger seat, her long arms behind her head, her bony knees propped against the door and glovebox. If she seemed in the grip of some impatience, some discontent – a sigh, a shift of her gangly body – she said nothing, and we drove in companionable silence, the sunlight streaming through the windows.

If there is one thing I remember best about those early days of my marriage, it is delight at my newfound ability to adjust to change, to make accommodations. I had wondered, before we wed, if I would be able to meet the needs of another person, never suspecting that I would have to meet the needs of two: my wife, and the old woman I had unexpectedly become. But I passed that test, and was proud, and that pride imbued everything I did with a golden glow, and made every small success seem like a great prize. I was delighted to find my love for my wife undiminished, and though our lovemaking lacked the urgency it had possessed on our wedding night – it was more an exercise in comfort than passion – it nevertheless seemed to fulfil some deep need in me, one I never knew I possessed. Whereas before I would be transported by sex, would lose myself in the softness of my wife's body and the quickness of her breath, now I felt that some well inside me, some pool of emotion that might otherwise go stagnant, was being stirred, and that the resulting waves would continue to wash through me long after the act was done. I was stimulated and renewed by these new feelings, and sensed that my wife, in her man's body, was finding satisfaction in the impulsive release, like the snap of a rubber band, that I once enjoyed. Making love with my wife, I could feel the parts of myself that being a man had made possible coming loose from their moorings, and drifting free. When I felt my wife's rough face between the dry skin of my breasts, I seemed to understand not only what it was to be a woman, but what it was to be the woman I myself had become. And when she pulled away, and I felt myself closing up in her wake, sealing myself off from her, and an ache ran through my bones, I understood what it was to be old.

They say that the first year of any marriage is the hardest; ours was no exception. We soon found ourselves arguing over the silliest things – where my medicine had gotten to, or to whom the razor blades belonged – problems that ought to have been resolved with a shrug of the shoulders, a peck on the cheek. Instead we shouted, pointed, spat. I accused my wife of sloth, of ingratitude, things of which I would never have accused her when she was a woman; likewise, she sneered at my stern nature, my professional ambition, qualities she had seemed to admire when I was a man. The fact was, we were the people we had always been, and though we could change for one another, there were limits. Our selves had boundaries which could not be crossed.

As the months passed, however, we gradually became aware that our fights were not about the medicine or razor blades; rather, they were about something neither of us wished to address: our mortality, the significance of which had been forced so cruelly upon us. 'Until death do us part,' we'd agreed months before – but what we hadn't anticipated was our failure to bear children, to create a family that we could be proud of, that we could hold up, in our declining years, as evidence of our significance here on earth. We were both disappointed, for which each blamed the other, however illogical this might have seemed. Was it I who had ground away my wife's strength, or she who had caused me to wither? When all two people have in the world is each other, there is no one else to accuse. As winter set in, our fights became more frequent and intense. We sensed a looming moment of crisis.

One cold morning, my wife was out shovelling the snow, as I watched her through the window: a weak old man, slouched over the handle, endangering her heart. I put on my coat and went out to help, and this touched off a fight: did I think she was so frail that she couldn't accomplish this simple task? Wasn't it already enough that I held the purse strings, must I dominate in everything? We stood in the cold, snow falling all around us, shouting insults, our terrible words rising, as clouds of steam, into the air. And then I went too far. 'Ungrateful bitch,' I said.

She slapped me. What else was she to do? She slapped me, and I fell. Anyone passing (there was no one) would have seen a old man striking an old woman to the ground, and this is what my wife saw, at last, as I lay groaning at her feet. Lying there, pain exploding in my hip, I forgave her everything: she had never known the strength of youth, she had never learned to control it. But I knew, as she knelt over my crumpled form, weeping, that she would never accept my forgiveness, that this guilt would remain with her to the grave – and so then would her resentment, at my fragility, at my pride, at my incapacity to be what she wished I was.

I spent some time in hospital, getting acquainted with my new hip, and when I hobbled, with my wife, over the threshold of our home, we agreed to work harder to make our marriage work. We would treat each other with greater respect, if necessary see a marriage counsellor. But, sadly, we never had the chance. I woke one morning to find my wife missing from the bed, and called out to her. When no answer came, I struggled into my robe and stumbled down the stairs. A chill met me at the bottom: the front door was open, and my wife lay on the threshold, her body curled, her breath shallow. She had bent over to get the newspaper and suffered a stroke.

She lasted a week in hospital, most of it in a coma. Her funeral was mercifully brief. 'Taken before his time,' the preacher said, and it was so. The next few weeks were filled with friendly faces, concerned neighbours, cousins, her parents and mine. But in time the visitors dried up, and I was left alone to contemplate what remained of my future. I had been supposed to die first – that was the unspoken agreement. But instead I had been left to live, and understood that I might live for some time.

You ask if I have any regrets. Had I to do it all again, would I never have married, would I have remained a man, and in the bloom of youth? It's difficult to say. If I'd been told on the altar that marriage would change me, would change my wife and me both, so drastically, perhaps I would have spurned it. Perhaps I would have turned and fled the church in shame. But what kind of life would I have had then? A longer life, maybe, a more conventional one, with all the rewards of conformity. (I had been, after all, a conventional kind of man.) But it would also have been a life of shame and doubt, a life in which I had been confronted by the uncertainty of life, and turned away in terror.

And perhaps it wouldn't have been longer, or conventional, or rewarding, after all. Maybe my insouciant, youthful confidence would have ruined me in the end. Even had I lived to the age I now appear to be, I might not have learned so much in all those years as I have learned in these few. Ultimately it doesn't matter that I am old, that I am a woman, and alone. I am who I have come to be through my own choices, which I made without compromise, and without fear. How many among us, as they near life's end, are able to say the same? And so, no. I have no regrets. I would do it all again.

David Almond

Slog's Dad

Spring had come. I'd been running round all day with Slog and we were starving. We were crossing the square to Myers' pork shop. Slog stopped dead in his tracks.

'What's up?' I said.

He nodded across the square.

'Look,' he said.

'Look at what?'

'It's me dad,' he whispered.

'Your dad?'

'Aye.'

I just looked at him.

'That bloke there,' he said.

'What bloke where?'

'Him on the bench. Him with the cap on. Him with the stick.'

I shielded my eyes from the sun with my hand and tried to see. The bloke had his hands resting on the top of the stick. He had his chin resting on his hands. His hair was long and tangled and his clothes were tattered and worn, like he was poor or like he'd been on a long journey. His face was in the shadow of the brim of his cap, but you could see that he was smiling.

'Slogger, man,' I said. 'Your dad's dead.'

'I know that, Davie. But it's him. He's come back again, like he said he would. In the spring.'

He raised his arm and waved.

'Dad!' he shouted. 'Dad!'

The bloke waved back.

'See?' said Slog. 'Howay.'

He tugged my arm.

'No,' I whispered. 'No!'

And I yanked myself free and I went into Myers', and Slog ran across the square to his dad.

Slog's dad had been a binman, a skinny bloke with a creased face and a greasy flat cap. He was always puffing on a Woodbine. He hung onto the back of the bin wagon as it lurched through the estate, jumped off and on, slung the bins over his shoulder, tipped the muck into the back. He was forever singing hymns – 'Faith of Our Fathers', 'Hail Glorious Saint Patrick', stuff like that. 'Here he comes again,' my mam would say as he bashed the bins and belted out 'Oh, Sacred Heart' at eight o'clock on a Thursday morning. But she'd be smiling, because everybody liked Slog's dad, Joe Mickley, a daft and canny soul.

First sign of his illness was just a bit of a limp, then Slog came to school one day and said, 'Me dad's got a black spot on his big toenail.'

'Just like *Treasure Island*, eh?' I said.

'What's it mean?' he said.

I was going to say death and doom, but I said, 'He could try asking the doctor.'

'He has asked the doctor.'

Slog looked down. I could smell his dad on him, the scent

of rotten rubbish that was always there. They lived just down the street from us, and the whole house had that smell in it, no matter how much Mrs Mickley washed and scrubbed. Slog's dad knew it. He said it was the smell of the earth. He said there'd be nowt like it in Heaven.

'The doctor said it's nowt,' Slog said. 'But he's staying in bed today, and he's going to hospital tomorrow. What's it mean, Davie?'

'How should I know?' I said.

I shrugged.

'It's just a spot, man, Slog!' I said.

Everything happened fast after that. They took the big toe off, then the foot, then the leg to halfway up the thigh. Slog said his mother reckoned his dad had caught some germs from the bins. My mother said it was all the Woodbines he puffed. Whatever it was it seemed they stopped it. They fitted a tin leg on him and sent him home. It was the end of the bins, of course. He took to sitting on the little garden wall outside the house. Mrs Mickley often sat with him and they'd be smelling their roses and nattering and smiling and swigging tea and puffing Woodbines.

He used to show off his new leg to passers-by.

'I'll get the old one back when I'm in Heaven,' he said.

If anybody asked was he looking for work, he'd laugh.

'Work? I can hardly bliddy walk.'

And he'd start in on 'Faith of Our Fathers' and everybody'd smile.

Then he got a black spot on his other big toenail, and they took him away again, and they started chopping at his other leg, and Slog said it was like living in a horror picture. When Slog's dad came home next he spent his days parked in a wheelchair in his garden. He didn't bother with tin legs: just pyjama bottoms folded over his stumps. He was quieter. He sat day after day in the summer sun among his roses staring out at the pebble-dashed walls and the red roofs and the empty sky. The Woodbines dangled in his fingers, 'Sacred Heart' drifted gently from his lips. Mrs Mickley brought him cups of tea, glasses of beer, Woodbines. Once I stood with Mam at the window and watched Mrs Mickley stroke her husband's head and gently kiss his cheek.

'She's telling him he's going to get better,' said Mam.

We saw the smile growing on Joe Mickley's face.

'That's love,' said Mam. 'True love.'

Slog's dad still joked and called out to anybody passing by.

'Walk?' he'd say. 'Man, I cannot even bliddy hop.'

'They can hack your body to a hundred bits,' he'd say. 'But they cannot hack your soul.'

We saw him shrinking. Slog told me he'd heard his mother whispering about his dad's fingers coming off. He told me about Mrs Mickley lifting his dad from the chair each night, laying him down, whispering her good nights, like he was a little bairn. Slog said that some nights when he was really scared, he got into bed beside them.

'But it just makes it worse,' he said. He cried. 'I'm bigger than me dad, Davie. I'm bigger than me bliddy dad!'

And he put his arms around me and put his head on my shoulder and cried.

'Slog, man,' I said as I tugged away. 'Howay, Slogger, man!'

One day late in August, Slog's dad caught me looking. He waved me to him. I went to him slowly. He winked.

'It's alreet,' he whispered. 'I know you divent want to

come too close.'

He looked down to where his legs should be.

'They tell us if I get to Heaven I'll get them back again,' he said. 'What d'you think of that, Davie?'

I shrugged.

'Dunno, Mr Mickley,' I said.

'Do you reckon I'll be able to walk back here if I do get them back again?'

'Dunno, Mr Mickley.'

I started to back away.

'I'll walk straight out them pearly gates,' he said. He laughed. 'I'll follow the smells. There's no smells in Heaven. I'll follow the bliddy smells right back here to the lovely earth.'

He looked at me. 'What d'you think of that?' he said.

Just a week later, the garden was empty. We saw Doctor Molly going in, then Father O'Mahoney, and just as dusk was coming on, Mr Blenkinsop, the undertaker.

The week after the funeral, I was heading out of the estate for school with Slog, and he told me, 'Dad said he's coming back.'

'Slogger, man,' I said.

'His last words to me. Watch for me in the spring, he said.'

'Slogger, man. It's just cos he was . . .'

'What?'

I gritted my teeth. 'Dying, man!'

I didn't mean to yell at him, but the traffic was thundering past us on the bypass. I got hold of his arm and we stopped.

'Bliddy dying,' I said more softly.

'Me mam says that and all,' said Slog. 'She says we'll have

to wait. But I cannot wait till I'm in Heaven, Davie. I want to see him here one more time.'

Then he stared up at the sky.

'Dad,' he whispered. 'Dad!'

I got into Myers'. Chops and sausages and bacon and black pudding and joints and pies sat in neat piles in the window. A pink pig's head with its hair scorched off and a grin on its face gazed out at the square. There was a bucket of bones for dogs and a bucket of blood on the floor. The marble counters and Billy Myers' face were gleaming.

'Aye aye, Davie,' he said.

'Aye,' I muttered.

'Saveloy, I suppose? With everything?'

'Aye. Aye.'

I looked out over the pig's head. Slog was with the bloke, looking down at him, talking to him. I saw him lean down to touch the bloke.

'And a dip?' said Billy.

'Aye,' I said.

He plunged the sandwich into a trough of gravy.

'Bliddy lovely,' he said. 'Though I say it myself. A shilling to you, sir.'

I paid him but I couldn't go out through the door. The sandwich was hot. The gravy was dripping to my feet.

Billy laughed.

'Penny for them,' he said.

I watched Slog get onto the bench beside the bloke.

'Do you believe there's life after death?' I said.

Billy laughed.

'Now there's a question for a butcher,' he said.

A skinny old woman came in past me.

'What can I do you for, pet?' said Billy. 'See you, Davie.'

He laughed.

'Kids!' he said.

Slog looked that happy as I walked towards them. He was leaning on the bloke and the bloke was leaning back on the bench grinning at the sky. Slog made a fist and face of joy when he saw me.

'It's Dad, Davie!' he said. 'See? I told you.'

I stood in front of them.

'You remember Davie, Dad,' said Slog.

The bloke looked at me. He looked nothing like the Joe Mickley I used to know. His face was filthy but it was smooth and his eyes were shining bright.

'Course I do,' he said. 'Nice to see you, son.'

Slog laughed.

'Davie's a bit scared,' he said.

'No wonder,' said the bloke. 'That looks very tasty.'

I held the sandwich out to him.

He took it, opened it and smelt it and looked at the meat and pease pudding and stuffing and mustard and gravy. He closed his eyes and smiled then lifted it to his mouth.

'Saveloy with everything,' he said. He licked the gravy from his lips, wiped his chin with his hand. 'Bliddy lovely. You got owt to drink?'

'No,' I said.

'Ha. He has got a tongue!'

'He looks a bit different,' said Slog. 'But that's just cos he's been . . .'

'Transfigured,' said the bloke.

'Aye,' said Slog. 'Transfigured. Can I show him your legs, Dad?'

The bloke laughed gently. He bit his saveloy sandwich. His eyes glittered as he watched me.

'Aye,' he said. 'Gan on. Show him me legs, son.'

And Slog knelt at his feet and rolled the bloke's tattered trouser bottoms up and showed the bloke's dirty socks and dirty shins.

'See?' he whispered.

He touched the bloke's legs with his fingers.

'Aren't they lovely?' he said. 'Touch them, Davie.'

I didn't move.

'Gan on,' said the bloke. 'Touch them, Davie.' His voice got colder. 'Do it for Slogger, Davie,' he said.

I crouched, I touched, I felt the hair and the skin and the bones and muscles underneath. I recoiled, I stood up again.

'It's true, see?' said Slog. 'He got them back in Heaven.'

'What d'you think of that, then, Davie?' said the bloke.

Slog smiled.

'He thinks they're bliddy lovely, Dad.'

Slog stroked the bloke's legs one more time then rolled the trousers down again.

'What's Heaven like, Dad?' said Slog.

'Hard to describe, son.'

'Please, Dad.'

'It's like bright and peaceful and there's God and the angels and all that . . .' The bloke looked at his sandwich. 'It's like having all the saveloy dips you ever want. With everything, every time.'

'It must be great.'

'Oh, aye, son. It's dead canny.'

'Are you coming to see Mam, Dad?' he said.

The bloke pursed his lips and sucked in air and gazed into the sky.

'Dunno. Dunno if I've got the time, son.'

Slog's face fell.

The bloke reached out and stroked Slog's cheek.

'This is very special,' he said. 'Very rare. They let it happen cos you're a very rare and special lad.'

He looked into the sky and talked into the sky.

'How much longer have I got?' he said, then he nodded. 'Aye. OK. OK.'

He shrugged and looked back at Slog.

'No,' he said. 'Time's pressing. I cannot do it, son.'

There were tears in Slog's eyes.

'She misses you that much, Dad,' he said.

'Aye. I know.' The bloke looked into the sky again. 'How much longer?' he said.

He took Slog in his arms.

'Come here,' he whispered.

I watched them hold each other tight.

'You can tell her about me,' said the bloke. 'You can tell her I love and miss her and all.' He looked at me over Slog's shoulder. 'And so can Davie, your best mate. Can't you, Davie? Can't you?'

'Aye,' I muttered.

Then the bloke stood up. Slog still clung to him.

'Can I come with you, Dad?' he said.

The bloke smiled.

'You know you can't, son.'

'What did you do?' I said.

'Eh?' said the bloke.

'What job did you do?'

The bloke looked at me, dead cold.

'I was a binman, Davie,' he said. 'I used to stink but I didn't mind. And I followed the stink to get me here.'

He cupped Slog's face in his hands.

'Isn't that right, son?'

'Aye,' said Slog.

'So what's Slog's mother called?' I said.

'Eh?'

'Your wife. What's her name?'

The bloke looked at me. He looked at Slog. He pushed the last bit of sandwich into his mouth and chewed. A sparrow hopped close to our feet, trying to get at the crumbs. The bloke licked his lips, wiped his chin, stared into the sky.

'Please, Dad,' whispered Slog.

The bloke shrugged. He gritted his teeth and sighed and looked at me so cold and at Slog so gentle.

'Slog's mother,' he said. 'My wife . . .' He shrugged again. 'She's called Mary.'

'Oh, Dad!' said Slog and his face was transfigured by joy. 'Oh, Dad!'

The bloke laughed. 'Ha! Bliddy ha!'

He held Slog by the shoulders.

'Now, son,' he said. 'You got to stand here and watch me go and you mustn't follow.'

'I won't, Dad,' whispered Slog.

'And you must always remember me.'

'I will, Dad.'

'And me, you and your lovely mam'll be together again one day in Heaven.'

'I know that, Dad. I love you, Dad.'

'And I love you.'

And the bloke kissed Slog, and twisted his face at me, then turned away. He started singing 'Faith of Our Fathers'. He walked across the square past Myers' pork shop, and turned down onto the High Street. We ran after him then and we looked down the High Street past the people and the cars but there was no sign of him, and there never would be again.

We stood there speechless. Billy Myers came to the doorway of the pork shop with a bucket of bones in his hand and watched us.

'That was me dad,' said Slog.

'Aye?' said Billy.

'Aye. He come back, like he said he would, in the spring.'

'That's good,' said Billy. 'Come and have a dip, son. With everything.'

Natalia Smirnova

The Garden Sketch

Translated by Nicholas Allen

Next to a half-tumbled-down villa with overgrown, moss-clad steps and a small tree growing from the roof, Sasha's husband bought a plot of land with a house and hired a gardener, with whom he set about grafting apple trees and trimming the hedges. Two hundred metres from the house began a health-resort zone with beaches and little cafés that sent music wafting on the evening air.

Sasha would have preferred a wood and a hammock strung between trees on their plot. The garden struck her as simple and logical, while a wood was full of mystery, but she had promised her husband she would spend the holiday with him, wood or no wood. When she and Tanya arrived, Sergei unfolded a sketch in front of them. It was a plan of the kitchen garden.

Sasha had little interest in vegetable allotments – or in the rest of the garden, for that matter. The next morning she and Tanya got ready to go to the beach. Tanya, who was thirty-three but looked twenty, slapped great dollops of moisturising cream on her face. As always, she was immaculately dressed in handmade Italian leather shoes and a light-coloured dress from Marks and Spencer.

Tanya was a computer programmer, often told ingenious untruths, shied away from housework and dreamed of getting married. Sasha tried to ignore her innocently dressed wiles because Tanya was a sweet thing really, affectionate and innocent, and she showed an almost canine devotion to her.

The nearest beach turned out to be for nudists. On the grass by the entrance lay a pale-skinned girl with a muddle of ginger curls, her legs lolling wide apart and her pubis shaven. A light green scarf covered her breasts. Sasha found this sight outrageously, blindingly beautiful. She slowed her pace and had another crafty peek. The girl was basking blissfully in the sun like a cat. Tanya walked with her eyes cast to the ground. She was such a stickler for decency, thought Sasha, what must she be feeling now?

They occupied a couple of vacant deckchairs. A naked young man wearing a small rucksack on his back and black socks and shoes scrunched past in the sand. Tanya got undressed, closed her eyes and fell straight asleep. How lucky, to be able to nod off in an instant as soon as you find a place to rest your head, Sasha thought. She surveyed her surroundings. More naked people sat nearby under an awning, chatting as they drank beer and wine. A stranger waved at her. She couldn't make out who it was because of the peak of her baseball cap, and she diffidently returned the greeting. The young man came over. 'Let's go and have a drink. They sell grappa here,' he said.

He was totally naked, half her age, strong in build and with perfectly proportioned shoulders and hips. They sat under the awning in wicker chairs that left imprints on their thighs. The waiter gave them the faint, all-comprehending smile characteristic of the east. They finished the grappa, drank white wine and ate succulent peaches. The juice ran down their hands, the wind picked up and wispy, colourless clouds raced across the sky. At the next table a portly man and a girl petted each other. The girl flashed looks at him through narrowed eyes, her black boots standing beside her like two dogs, with no other clothing in sight.

'Shall we go for a dip?' asked the young man, whose name was Stas.

He helped Sasha down the slippery clay steps and immediately put his arms round her in the water. He pressed his face into the nape of her neck and inhaled her scent. They stood for a while and then swam in the warm, filmy water, which was like green layers of velvet. On the other bank he lay her down on the grass and had his way with her. Grasshoppers chirped, clouds drifted in the sky and her back inflamed in blisters from the nettles beneath. She felt nothing apart from the weight and soft coolness of his body, his firm buttocks cupped in her hands.

She returned to Tanya, who opened her eyes, happy and blank from sleep.

'Was I asleep long?' she asked.

'No.'

While she was asleep, Sasha had drunk wine, swum to the other bank and given herself to a stranger in the grass. Was it a long time? she wondered. No, it happened almost instantly and simply, the effect of summer perhaps. Stas sat nearby, not looking at her. Just another Russian male, she thought, plenty of ambition, imagination and plans, but still just a primate. He'd fed and watered her, screwed her in the bushes and lost interest.

Some friends came up to Stas. One wearing suede shoes

asked: 'You ready to go?' Hiding a smirk, the young man – a shaven-headed athletic type – glanced at Sasha.

'How old are you then, thirty?'

'Why, thank you,' she replied, smiling, but was then glad to be taken by a feeling of indifference.

Stas grabbed his jeans and T-shirt. Not dressing, he stopped as he passed.

'Perhaps I could get your telephone number?'

Sasha thought for a second and shook her head. Nonetheless she experienced a flush of joy. Her eyes still twinkling, she climbed onto Tanya's old Honda and they drove home. It took them three minutes.

Her husband, the gardener and the neighbour Vera were having a heated discussion concerning what to do with the stones by the path.

'So the ladies have been sunbathing, have they?' asked Vera, her eyes boring into them as they passed.

Didn't even say hello, the old bitch, thought Sasha angrily. The husband works while the wife plays, and that's all this one-track-minded hag sees. She nodded curtly and went through to the garden. There were three wild stawberries growing by the fence. She popped them into her mouth one by one. Then she went into the house and put on some trousers before clambering into the overgrown raspberry canes. How tender and sweet the berries were! If raspberries are not ripe they taste like grass, if they are overripe they are muck with the texture of a damp floor cloth. Yet so beautiful, like a woven basket, she mused.

Tanya called them all to lunch. They ate mashed potato and carrot-and-onion soup as the wind played with the lace curtains on the window. Tanya bit into a tomato, recoiling with a giggle as it sent a jet of juice and seeds into her eye.

'I met a naked boy on the beach,' said Sasha suddenly.

'Hanging out with youngsters now?' said Sergei, narrowing his eyes. 'Actually, you look really well.'

'So do you.'

They both looked pretty good. His strong, sun-bronzed shoulders gleamed like onion skin. Sergei ate only fresh food, looked after his health and loved working in the garden. We look like last year's apples stored in wax, their shine still preserved, thought Sasha. Stuffed with mashed potatoes and no one knows it. At least, not yet.

A wasp buzzed around her head and Sasha froze. It even seemed to have a smell, like glowing hot metal. She felt the wasp's searing sting sink into the nape of her neck and an acute pain almost knocked her from her seat. The striped gladiator had rent her skull in two. She cried out, clutched her head and then suddenly relaxed, as discomfort yielded to pleasure: a second of pain, then a blissful sensation flooded her body, as if she were being cut into thin strips with a scalpel, and how delicious it felt.

She left the table and went to her room. Tanya followed and sat at the foot of her bed.

'It seems I missed something,' she said. 'Slept through everything like always. That redhead with the spread legs gave me such a fright on the beach that I fell straight asleep.'

'The beach, yes,' said Sasha, engrossed in thought. 'Your desires have free reign there. But it's not for me, I'm too old for this. I just realised that everything happened too fast in life. As if I marry today and I'm an old woman by tomorrow, or hear the bell for class and straight after the last class ends. Girls blossom, decorate the world, learn to kiss and fall in love. Women love their men, tend the house and raise the children. And then what? You still have twenty or thirty years ahead of you, but for a woman, it's already the end. What are you supposed to do?'

Tanya feigned a look of heartfelt concern. You're a strong woman, you'll think of something, get by somehow.'

Sasha look at her pityingly. What a silly little fool. She doesn't understand that some things are insurmountable. No matter what sort of a person you are, there are things you simply cannot overcome. And the more of a fighter you are, the harder it is to learn humility.

Sasha had often thought about humility since she started to take confession in a church at Sergiev Posad. Father Nikolai called torment and suffering 'a visitation by God', and spoke of trials and tribulations as 'beneficial'. To him, tragedies were as common and natural as tea drinking.

After their own tea drinking by the samovar that evening, Tanya said her goodbyes and promised to come back the day after next, when they'd go and do this beach properly.

But the day after next everything went the same way. Tanya fell asleep as soon as her head touched the deckchair.

Stas came up to Sasha. 'Why weren't you here yesterday?' he asked. His question found its answer in a sweet stab of pain in the nape of Sasha's neck.

'A wasp stung me.'

'Come with me, I've got something for insect stings.'

She got up obediently and felt she was trailing after him like a goat on a tether.

The skinhead friend appeared from somewhere with a smirk on his shiny, sun-tanned face.

'Got all dressed up did you?' Sasha asked, nodding at the

heavy gold chain round his neck.

'There's a dame here I want to like me,' he replied, looking pointedly in her eyes. He could barely stand still, every muscle and sinew of his powerful body twitched and rippled. She walked past him, feeling his gaze on her back.

They trudged across the shifting sand to the log boathouse. It was cool and empty inside except for a large bed, a chest of drawers and a mirror. A lifebelt hung on one of the gleaming whitewashed walls and the place smelled of fish. Stas drew back the bedspread to reveal clean sheets.

'Are you the boat attendant?' she asked, as it occurred to her that she knew nothing about him.

'Actually, I'm a website designer. My friends live here.'

He slipped her bikini strap from her shoulder, looked at her and slipped off the other. She continued to look round at the room.

'So this is the place where all the dates take place?' she said.

'No, it's the place of romantic passions.' He grinned.

So light and cool here. He was already caressing her thighs. Again she felt the stab of pain in her neck, and then that pleasurable buzz creeping through her. His tongue was quick, deft, expert.

'The first time was a test run,' he warned. 'Now it's for real'.

The sun was setting when they left the boathouse and its windows glowed scarlet in the dipping rays. Sasha could not feel her body as she left and clung onto his hand, not wanting to release it. It was as if she had been grafted onto him, incapable of letting go. In her ears she could hear the squeak-squeak of the wooden bed, like the sound of the sea.

A man with a skipper beard sat beside Tanya, his arm

around her waist. She was smiling at him uncertainly.

'We're going to the café, I'm hungry,' said Sasha and took Stas by the hand again. The man looked at her with surprise but didn't pull his hand back.

The café hummed with music and was full of young people.

'Hey, they're all gay,' she exclaimed, taken aback.

'Wait here a minute, I'll just get some cigarettes.' As Stas walked off a girl came over to Sasha, smiled and motioned her to dance. Her blouse slipped down from one satiny shoulder and then the other as she moved. What an absolute darling. Sasha found it funny when their breasts touched, and laughed. Stas reappeared but he didn't like their dance and sat down at the next table, lit up and covered one eye with his hand.

'I'm Nastya,' said the girl, beaming at Sasha. 'Listen, you've got fantastic skin! What do you do for a living?'

'I'm a journalist,' said Sasha, taking a rest from the never-ending Gloria Gaynor song. She would have tired long ago were it not for the stranger's occasional touch.

'Teach me to dance like you,' said the girl.

'I'm not here alone.'

'You're with Stas?' she giggled. 'He's always got someone different. Another day, another ejaculation.' She flashed a smile, Sasha forced one in return, turned and left the dance circle to join Stas.

'Listen, I don't know where to take you,' he said with a sigh. 'The boatman doesn't let anyone in there at night.'

'Let's go to my place. I have a flat.'

He took her hand and they went up to the main road and waved down a car. It was a thirty-minute drive to the city and they sat in silence all the way. The fire in her slowly rose again and in the lift they inexorably began to embrace.

He slept on his belly with outstretched legs, looking like a golden statue on the pink sheets, and Sasha remembered the alley of ancient gods in the Crimean resort of Simeiz. In the morning they drank fresh, un-sugared coffee and chatted, Sasha in her nightdress.

'About twenty years ago there was a summer theatre where this beach is now,' she told him. 'They used to put on plays and singers and showmen would perform. In the café I saw an old piece of scenery wrapped around the transformer.'

'Stop it.' Stas put down his cup and lit a cigarette. 'Never mind the trip down memory lane. And take that horrible thing off,' he said, nodding to her blue, long-sleeved, high-collared nightdress.

'It's English,' she protested.

'It's old-maidish.'

Sasha fell silent, angered but thoughtful.

'Don't you get the feeling we are doing something improper?' she asked.

Stas raised his hands and wordlessly contorted his face for a minute, pursing and un-pursing his lips in fake indignation. Finishing his pantomime, he asked quietly: 'Are you a believer then?'

'Yes,' Sasha looked him in the eyes, resolving not to be distracted by their colour and reflection.

'So what exactly do you believe in?'

'That I must find the meaning of my life myself. Up to the age of thirty I was a dancer in a variety show, dancing at night like a moth. Then I studied a long time. Now . . .'

He waved his hand dismissively.

'I'm not blind. Maybe leave the reminiscences for another

time. It's silly.'

'No, I shall tell you now,' said Sasha stubbornly.

There is no meaning of life, Stas assured her, that's just an error in consciousness and an artificial creation. Harmony is the only thing there is. Coincidence with place, time and function. Timeliness, appropriateness, effectiveness.

They got into a heated argument, shouted and waved their arms at each other. Then they tired and everything took a turn in the other direction.

'For example, you and I are not appropriate,' Sasha told him. 'Everyone notices it and drops hints. Your skinhead friend asked straight away how old I am, remember?'

'He's a moron and you're the sad clown,' he said. 'I'm not going to comfort you, but rather warn you that I'll end up leaving you anyway. Just don't cry to me about it later.'

'How do you expect me not to cry!' shrieked Sasha, leaping up. 'You're a Casanova, aren't you – new girls all the time!'

'Is that right?' Stas looked surprised. 'Who told you that? That little tart in the café? That's because she wanted you. I'm no Casanova. I'm the last romantic, you just remember that.'

'If you intend to leave, then do it now. It's for the best, it really is,' said Sasha. She sat, waiting, her eyes fixed on him.

He didn't move.

'I don't know why you're carrying on like this. What are you boasting about, your experience, that you were born eighteen years before me? What good does that do you then, do tell me?'

Many things became clear to Sasha that morning. Like breaking up with him would be unbearably painful and getting closer to him impossible and no less painful. They went back to the beach together. Everything she saw there that day seemed strikingly clear, as if she were looking through freshly washed glass, unsullied with mud or dust. Had the world suddenly shed the patina that had obscured it before, or had her sight become sharper and every joy slipped into focus? Climbing into fresh sheets, racing along on a bicycle, watching butterflies flutter, inhaling the scent of flowers, playing with a child, feeling a cat amble lazily along your back. How much happiness there is mixed into everything; no one even knows how much. As much as you can take in.

The scene on the beach was unchanged. The man with the skipper beard leant over Tanya and tenderly stroked her back. Tanya saw Sasha and adopted a look of deep concern.

'Where have you been? Sergei couldn't find you. I said you went to the dance and that it went on all night. Call him.'

'No, let's go home.'

Ten minutes later she sat before her sullen husband and, detesting herself, babbled out the first lies that came into her head, regardless of the consequences. When she finished, she breathed out deeply, as if casting off a heavy weight.

'Don't you want a divorce then?' she asked.

'Absolutely not.'

Sergei stepped down from the veranda and picked up the hoe, unwilling to speak. It would be better if he hit her, thought Sasha. But no, that would be too dramatic and he didn't like dramatic gestures, only measured ones. He preferred to conserve his energies for things to come.

Sasha stood silently behind him, at a loss what to say. She

looked at his swarthy back, the skin glistening with sweat. For twenty-two years he had lain beside her at night with his hand on her thigh. He would say her skin was smooth as kid gloves and her eyes were like malachite. Her eyes were in fact anything but malachite, khaki like bottle glass, the colour of olives or sometimes tobacco, but never malachite. Maybe he meant they were like stone? Sasha stood a while and then went in the house to wash the curtains.

Inside, Tanya excitedly told her that the 'skipper' had offered to marry her. Her dream had begun to come true.

'Maybe the beach is the place where the most important things really happen,' Sasha wondered out loud. Tanya lapsed into thought.

After supper they went out for a walk but as they turned onto the road they ran into Stas.

'Are you avoiding me?' he asked, and without waiting for an answer took a photograph from his jeans pocket and showed it to her.

'Why did you take it?' she asked.

He didn't reply and put the photo back in his pocket.

Sasha couldn't help but smile. Well how about that? He stole her picture from an album – and not just any photo but one of her when she was twenty-two. He'll sleep with it beside him and love this girl with the joyful eyes. Her father was still alive then, she hadn't started dancing in the variety show and was just finishing university. Only later did everything turn sour. But at twenty-two everything was great, just great.

'Why didn't you come back? You promised.'

'And what is there to do there? Laze around pointlessly while little brats hit on you?'

She continued down the road, her head bowed. Stas caught up and grabbed her by the arm. Tanya vanished in the twilight. As well as falling asleep on the spot she could also disappear if something was not to her liking. Tanya had many ways of defending and rescuing herself.

'What's the matter with you?' Stas drew Sasha close and looked in her eyes. 'Are you crying?'

'Why did you tell me this morning you would leave me? OK, you will leave, but why tell me?'

'I'm sorry, forgive me, I'm a fool.' He put his arms round her and pressed her head to his breast. 'My darling girl.'

Sasha pressed herself even closer into him.

'OK, let's say I'm not past it yet. But a butterfly still can't become a doll again, do you understand?' she said.

'What rubbish is this now?'

'. . . And the dragonfly sang the whole wonderful summer long, and before it knew it, winter had set in. Do you get it now? Winter is setting in . . .'

Unable to contain herself, Sasha burst into sobs. He held her close and stroked her head.

'But what should I do?' His voice was muffled and far away. 'What can I do? If I want you, I want to sleep with you, live with you, stroke your hair. You dance better than anyone else here, you eat quickly, earn well, can afford a lot. Your skin is like silk, you're the best lover a man might hope to find. Why am I saying all this, I even find myself ridiculous?' said Stas, by now almost talking to himself.

'And I'll die eighteen years before you,' said Sasha.

'Is that supposed to be a joke, stop it,' he said sharply. 'How can you even think about this? That won't happen – I'll draw your portrait and you'll never die.'

'I already did die and you're a fool with damaged instincts. Can't even find yourself a girl.'

'I can find a hundred if I want, but none of them are right. The wrong kind of music.'

He's crazy, thought Sasha angrily, and wiped her tears. They're all maniacs on this beach: narcissists, exhibitionists, pederasts and pensioner-fetishists. Why did she mention divorce to Sergei? She must be going mad. Maybe its contagious? She'd have to talk to Tanya about it, she's one who is definitely not mad. Sasha strode off towards the house without turning to Stas. He stayed where he was, standing in the shadow of a tree.

Tanya was sitting on the veranda and watching the moths. She turned and watched anxiously as Sasha paced furiously up and down. To be on the safe side, she retreated silently into her shell like a snail.

'Tanya, do you think this guy on the beach was serious when he proposed to you?'

Tanya sighed with relief. 'Of course not. I never even thought so for a minute.'

'So it was a joke then?'

'Why? When he said it he believed it. But who marries a guy who hits on you on the beach? It's all just dancing and flirting, just a game,' explained Tanya, seeing that Sasha didn't understand. 'I enjoy it, so does he,' she said slowly, like a teacher talking to first formers, impressing every word upon her. 'It's fun to dream of marriage, children.'

'But it's not real,' interrupted Sasha.

Tanya's eyes widened with surprise. 'You think it can be different? That with you it's different?'

'Yes,' said Sasha hesitatingly.

Tanya shrugged.

'And that's better is it? You were both shouting out there on the road, I could hear it from here. It sounded like you were crying.'

Tanya winced at the mere mention and Sasha was plain horrified. How could she have lowered herself to this, fighting so the whole neighbourhood could hear?

'You're right, it's just one awful mess. *Summer, sun, heat and ease, naked bodies, do as you please* . . . This has to stop, hasn't it?' she said.

'That's up to you, but I'm still going to go there. Maybe I'll keep on going there for a long time, maybe always.'

'Until you grow old?' asked Sasha in surprise.

'As an old woman too. What else do I have, if we're brutally honest?' said Tanya.

'I can't do it.' Sasha bit her lip.

'Because of your arrogant pride.'

I'm lying to myself, thought Sasha. Tanya isn't lying but I am, as if I have something more than this. Neither of us has anything, we are lonely like travellers in the desert. Sometimes we encounter another lone person and we're overjoyed. But after this brief happiness we part and go our own way. Everything we have is fake, a substitute, just cheap trinkets.

Sasha went to her husband, sat down at the table opposite him and clutched her head with her fingers.

'Sergei, I want to join a nunnery. I really do.'

He slowly rocked on his chair and looked her in the eyes.

'A couple of days ago you said you met a boy at the beach. Then you vanished from home and when you came back you talked about divorce. Now you want to go into a nunnery. So what was the point of your life then? To go and pull all these disgraceful, ridiculous stunts?'

'Listen. Our life together has reached its end. The kids grew up and left, I'm not interested in the garden. Let me go, I beg you.'

'We are talking about different things,' he said. 'You were always very self-possessed, with full control over your body and mind. Just get a grip on yourself, OK? Being an idiot doesn't suit you.'

Sasha stood up, tied a sweater around her neck and went out onto the village road where the lampposts were overgrown in thick foliage. She walked long and far, dogs barked in the darkness behind her. Suddenly a man appeared from the shadows and blocked her path. It was the athlete with the suede shoes from the beach, now filthy drunk. She didn't recognise him immediately in clothes. He took a step forward and pulled her towards him, smothering her with the stink of vodka.

'Got you, didn't I? I've been looking for you for ages. Come on, get down there and get busy, now!' he said, starting to force her onto her knees in front of him. Sasha twisted and punched him in the face, connecting with his jaw. His teeth clattered together and he stumbled with the shock.

'Aah, you bitch,' he cursed, lunging at her and catching hold of the sweater tied round Sasha's neck as she was about to slip away. She couldn't throw it off in time and once again he had her, blocking her way.

'Tell me, is Stas better than me? How is he better?' he mumbled, lifting her off the ground by her armpits. 'Me and him had a threesome once, and I'm better.'

Sasha had no option but to kick him between the legs and

break away with all her strength and run. He yelped but after a couple of seconds was in hot pursuit, pounding after her. His shadow drew steadily closer, then came the sound of a heavy fall and a struggle. Sasha heard someone groan in pain but kept running like mad until she reached the house and fell in a heap on the veranda steps, gasping for breath. Tanya helped her up and took her inside. Her arms and legs were trembling; her body was bathed in hot sweat. Sasha went to bed but was haunted all night by shouts, moans and wailing ambulance sirens.

The next morning she heard Vera's loud voice.

'We're surrounded by proles here, bums. Someone got stabbed last night. They sent a van from the morgue to take the body away. A young man, handsome too. Carved him up with a knife, the swines. That skinhead guy should have been in jail long ago. All covered in tattoos he was.'

Sasha looked at the neighbour, then at Tanya. Tanya looked lost, not knowing what to say, then she nodded and bowed her head.

Without a word Sasha got her things to go to the beach. Vera was still holding forth on the veranda as she left. Sasha caught a few words: 'I hate teachers, they are all corrupt!'

'I won't stand any more of this,' said Sasha as a vein began to pulse on her temple. 'My mother was a teacher.'

'Oh do excuse me!' said Vera in mock apology. 'Aren't we irritable today . . .'

'Go home, you have no business here,' interrupted Sasha. Vera exchanged a glance with Tanya, stood up and left haughtily.

Sasha barely noticed the walk to the beach, although it seemed to be windy. Undressing, she swam to the other bank. She remembered where it first happened and found the spot immediately, lay down and sobbed loudly. The grass under her face quickly grew wet and salty. An hour or more passed before she swam back. Yellow leaves floated in the dark green water and she swam together with them, lamenting their passing, summer's passing, everything that had been lost. Life seemed like an enormous expanse to her, thrown open in her time of loss, but she had no more tears to shed.

She was met in Sergiev Posad by Father Nikolai and confessed her long absence.

'A friend of mine died,' she said. 'I loved him, although I didn't want to.'

'This is a trial sent to you,' the priest began, but the vein on her temple suddenly pulsed again wildly. How good they all were at giving things names! Trial, transgression, confession, penance – give it a name and it's taken care of, the essence slips away, tightly swaddled in the label, the colours fade, life dies, turns to bronze, turns to stone, crumbles to dust. Tanya also found a name for it: she called it a game.

'Forgive me, I lied,' she interrupted. 'He was my lover. This was no idle indulgence of the passions of the flesh, but the quenching of desires. I could have died not knowing what I now know. It's better to live with open eyes, is that not so, Father? And is not actual life about fulfilling our main desires? A hungry person must first be fed, then set on the path of righteousness, is that not so?'

Rummaging in the folds of his robe, the Priest pulled out a mobile telephone and dialled a number. It was time to return the lost sheep to the herd. Father Nikolai and the Mother Superior of the Iversk nunnery agreed on a year's penance.

The first thing Sasha saw in the yard of the nunnery was a spade and a rake. The 'kitchen garden plan' flashed through her mind.

She asked if she could do translations during her stay as she had studied ancient Greek at university, but they allowed her only physical work. She was also not permitted to walk by the river. She was, indeed, drawn to the water, painfully so, and she craved to sink into the black depths forever so that not even the sound of the ringing belfry could reach her. But gradually Sasha was drawn into the even rhythm of worship, meals in the refectory and hard work. The days melded into one endless, long, empty year. At night she would cry for him and there was no end to the tears that came afresh each time. The people around her seemed bodiless and faceless, but apart from having permanently swollen eyes she barely differed from them.

Conversations with the Mother Superior were an ordeal, repentance did not come and nor could it. There is nothing on earth one cannot make one's peace with, she would be told, everything is the work of the Lord's hand. But Sasha did not apply herself hard enough to come to terms with death and she did not understand how others were able to. Take Tanya, who could fall asleep on the beach when she could not. She sincerely tried to learn humility but the only thing she gained was a state of calm that felt alien to her, heavy, leaden like a bullet.

A year later Sergei came to collect Sasha as agreed. He treated her delicately as he would a sick person, and slightly guiltily. He took her home and showed her the long-since completed kitchen garden and was very happy. Sasha suddenly felt happy herself, took the hoe and started to help, so natural had this work become for her in the past year. She tied a scarf around her head and even started to sing, occasionally glancing up at the black clouds gathering in the sky.

A stream of people passed the house on their way back from the beach as the storm was about to break. There came a clap of thunder and a flash of lightening and Sasha joyfully turned her face to catch the first raindrops. After a few minutes rivulets ran down her face and she screwed up her eyes and savoured the sensation, thinking that just as water always finds its own course, so does life stubbornly rise over death.

'Hey! Hey!' came a shout from the fence. Sasha turned round. Stas was standing by the gate. She crossed herself and shut her eyes, then opened them again. He was smiling! Sasha cautiously approached. He was in shorts; a terrible scar ran across his chest, and she couldn't take her eyes off this crookedly sewn, furrowed line. As her throat constricted, Sasha had never felt greater pity and tenderness in her life than she did now for this hacked up body.

'You lost weight,' he said. 'Your eyes got bigger too. By seventy you'll be quite a beauty. So where did you get to, you traitor? Left me to die on the road! It's just as well Vasya sobered up and called an ambulance.'

Stas turned and squinted at some point on the horizon and continued talking to himself. 'I thought of her every day God gave me. To find my own, beloved woman only to lose her so stupidly. Where were you?' He looked at her out of the corner of his eye.

'I . . . I thought you were dead.'

'Who told you that? Who?'

She was confused for a minute, then remembered with

difficulty. 'Tanya.'

'That's what you thought, did you? How could I die if I wanted to live with you? Even now I want this more than anything in the world. If you were for real you'd pack your things and leave. Right now.'

He fell silent, lowered his head and looked at her from under his brow.

'Well, is that too much for you to do?'

'Too much for me?' Sasha forced herself to look up from the scar and licked her now dry lips. 'Of course not.'

She only had a bag, haircomb and toothbrush in the house. As she dashed in to get them the pouring rain stopped as suddenly as it started. She came down from the veranda; the garden was washed, the world seemed clean, clear and unsullied.

Vera waved at her from over the fence. Sasha went over.

'You know about this husband of yours?' she whispered. 'He lives with Tanya. They got together while you were away.'

'Never mind, it's all just a game. It's not real,' said Sasha.

She went out of the gate and walked with Stas up the wet road. The stones on the verge shone like new shoes in the hallway. The wind shook the branches of the trees and the last drops of rain fell.

Margaret Wilkinson

Scarfman

I want to run, but I take my sweet time crossing the room. My heart's already beating quickly which ain't good for my health. Slowly, I stoop, knees creaking. Nice envelope wedged neatly under the door. Smooth. Blank. I pick it up. Drop it. Pick it up again. Drop it. I can't get a grip. Finally I get a grip. Holding on tightly, I resist the urge to tear it open. The hell with that. I tear it open. It's open. Inside, a single sheet of paper and the name Rosalie Ossipovna-Aromat, written in a familiar heavy hand. What kind of name's that? I put on my glasses. Maybe it's a joke. I take off my glasses. Turn the sheet of paper over. On the other side, one word: 'pronto'.

My tongue's dry and thick. It's an effort to swallow. I fold the paper into quarters, eighths, sixteenths, creasing each fold with my thumbnail, then set it alight in the bathroom sink. On my way back to bed, I stop at the window, raise the blinds, and run my fingers across the glass. Men in hardhats swarm over a construction site. A mechanical digger sways. Quickly I look away. There's a little crack in the linoleum beneath my feet. As I stare at it, it begins to widen. I grab the headboard, shut my eyes. Finally I'm able to lie down. Why am I lying down? I should be getting dressed. Make an effort, I tell myself. Get up. Get dressed. Get out. Lose a little beef.

Buy a suit. I got suits. Suits I can't wear. Nice pinstripes with matching waistcoats, a drawer full of scarves. Ah scarves. Fat wallets and scarves. A guy can dream, can't he? I toss from one end of the mattress to the other. A luminous clock on the night table reads 6 p.m. The light's draining from the sky. Rosalie? I touch the hot sheets tenderly. What have you done?

I turn. Rabbit-punch the pillow. One-two. One-two. If the Hypnotiser wants her whacked, she's whacked. The Hypnotiser's my hero. A philosopher of muscle, he still manages 50 chest elevators a day, plus squat thrusts and chair lifts. The man's a physical genius. He carries a short-nosed .32 and flies an American flag from the balcony of his condo. Everyone's got a condo, these days, except you-know-who. You-know-who's got a book on holes hidden under his bed.

'Take a rest,' the Hypnotiser told me. So I took a rest that wasn't so restful.

Once upon a time, I was the man. Scarfman. One of four sleek-suited executives, that's what we called ourselves. 'Executives.' Honest to God. Then one day, the sky comes down like a fist and the ground beneath my feet goes soft. I start seeing holes everywhere. Out on the street, I look drunk, weaving around those lousy holes no one else knows are there. I understand they aren't real. But I'm frightened by the fact that I'm seeing them in such detail, seeing right down to the electricity cables, telephone cables, gas mains, water mains and waste pipes. While I'm looking at holes, a hot-shot rival muscles in. What's his name? Fank? A face like a young horse. He's built too. Fank? Fank? Why isn't he called Frank?

Rosalie Ossipovna-Aromat sounds like a foreign dame. I still can't figure it. The Hypnotiser don't do politics. It had to be personal. It always was with dames. Dames like Sunny. I took a lot of crap when I was married to Sunny.

There's Sunny in a beige cashmere sweater, like Grace Kelly. My Sunny. Love bites on her neck. She's laughing, feeding pretty-boy Fank bar nuts, one by one. They're sitting in the back of the bar, near the pay phones, in the darkest corner, thinking they're alone. Then Sunny looks up, sees me.

She hurries over, tries to grasp my arm. Suddenly everything makes sense. The telephone ringing in the middle of the night. The way she pours coffee, not looking at me like she used to. Once upon a time, I gave her the story of my life. We sat under a tree covered in pale pink cherry blossoms. With every breeze, blossoms wafted around us. I wanted no secrets from Sunny. Pulling a serious face, I traced the thread of my life to a childhood incident in the woods.

'What woods?' she asked.

'Some woods.'

The real truth involved a man who wore a scarf around his neck in all weathers. A friend of the family. Call him uncle. Uncle leans over, the ends of his scarf dangling. Sunny hardly struggled at all.

Now and again, I think about Sunny in candlelight. Sunny with a Chihuahua.

I brought her pillow with me when I moved in here, wrapped in a dry-cleaning bag. When I brush it with my elbow, the plastic moans. I swing my legs over the side of the bed, barely missing the hole opening up in the carpet. My stomach rocks. I bend over. Everything's fine, I tell myself, which is not the truth. I reach under the bed for my book. *The Book of Caves. Caves are commonly formed in areas of limestone.* It's a big book with glossy pages. Best book I ever had. *Made of calcium carbonate, limestone dissolves in carbonic acid, naturally present in rainwater. This acidic water trickles through cracks in the stone, eventually causing deep holes to appear.* I cross my legs. My foot starts to shake.

Dressed in a faded black sweatshirt and matching sweat pants, I avoid the full-length mirror hanging on the back of my closet door. Built like a light heavyweight, all muscle in my prime, I had clothes tailored to flatter my frame. Dark suit. Dark tie. Florsheims on my feet. I flaunted my size, bluffed my way though a million confrontations. Now, a feeling for the sharp suits I can no longer fit into comes over me. Kneeling in front of the scarf drawer, I dither. Why go in disguise? I'm not Scarfman. I'm Ernest Goldfarb. No I'm not. I'm Scarfman. I find a good scarf, a strong and supple scarf, and fold it carefully. I don't carry a gun. A long silk scarf's my trademark. My MO. Slowly I tie the scarf around my neck. I'm lethal with a scarf. One slip, I'm a dead man. My hands tremble. A little flutter. That's all. A shaky glug of cold coffee and I'm all right again.

Before leaving the house, I spend time in the bathroom, fixing my hair. I take an Alka-Seltzer, a Theragran stress tablet and a tablespoon of extra strength Maalox. What I need's a Dexedrine, or whatever it is hotheads swallow these days to stay alert. I don't take the elevator. Instead, I head for the stairs. One flight later, I'm panting. I duck out of the stairs and ring for the elevator. The elevator comes. It's empty. I enter, push G for ground floor. Crummy building has an elevator and a ground floor. Catching a glimpse of myself in a piece of sliding-door chrome, I bounce my fingers gently through my hair, sculpted into a tall grey pompadour.

When the elevator stops and the doors hiss open, I step out, eyes jumping from side to side. Last chance, I tell myself.

Out on the street, I'm walking in my usual staggering way, weaving between the holes. It's better if you don't look directly at them. As a boy, I was always looking down. I once found a diamond ring on the pavement. My mother started kvelling, but it turned out to be only an industrial diamond called a zircon. Old people, bent and doddering, gaze at the ground. It's a sign that they're searching for what's been lost: energy, beauty, health, possessions, memories. I try and fail to ignore an ache in the back of my throat and along my jaw. A few limp clouds hang in the muggy sky. I hope it don't rain. I hate that lousy rainwater. Spending almost all the money I've got, I buy a box of cigars, a carton of cigarettes, and a disposable lighter at a newsstand. I'll smoke myself to death, if I fail with Rosalie. I go to the usual drop (weaving between the holes, it takes forever) and pick up the address and two keys. Rosalie, I think. Rosalie, Rosalie, Rosalie. I imagine a beautiful, headstrong woman with a samovar. Probably pissed off the Hypnotiser bigtime.

'Watch it, asshole.' A man heading for the garment district, wheeling a trolley full of clothes wrapped in dry-cleaning plastic, bumps into me.

Instinctively I bunch my big fists. I still have the moves. The rapid-fire reactions. The instincts. But I back off. I got more important fish to fry. I got Rosalie.

There's a fresh breeze coming off the river now. It feels good. It feels right. Quickly I review my strategy. In and out. I don't need much time. I'm experienced. I got the whole operation in my head. The Scarfman's back, I tell myself. The man with the golden scarf. In fact, I've got scarves in all colours. I touch my hair with my fingers, lightly confirming its big shape. Nothing to worry about. Darting between dawdling pedestrians, I pick up the pace. Crossing the street while the DON'T WALK's flashing, I decide to play it cool. Play it cool like peach-fuzz Fank. Rosalie, I tease, I'm coming. I feel so good, I take a chance and look down at the pavement. Nothing! No holes, just asphalt glowing in the dusky light. Rashly I dump my smokes in a trashcan. Let some other poor slob get lucky. I have the funny feeling things are going to start improving from now on.

The exterior door's locked, but I have the key ready and waiting. Inside, there's a long smooth corridor lit with fluorescent tubes leading to a row of mailboxes. I look left, right, left again, but the lobby's empty. Gloves on, I hurry up the stairs. None of my normal huffing and puffing. My feet feel light. No cold sweats. Zero fear. A moment of gut-fluttering joy, but I keep my face totally frozen searching for her apartment. A thick buff-coloured door. The name Ossipovna-Aromat stamped on a strip of plastic under the peephole. I let myself noiselessly in with the second key. The blinds are down. One light's burning, making a high-wattage circle on the parquet. I unfurl the scarf and creep forward.

But Rosalie's not there. She's supposed to be there. Am I too early? Or too late? I can't believe my crap luck. Grudgingly I slip into the hall closet to wait.

In the cave of the closet, there's nothing to do but think. An hour goes by. Rosalie's closet smells like mothballs. I begin to feel light-headed. Then I get chokey, like I swallowed a hair. It's dark, but not entirely dark. A small amount of light seeps around the edges of the door. For a long time I sit staring at it, until the whole closet shifts in space and I feel as if I'm gazing up from the bottom of a tomb. My heart misses beat. An old fur coat, like my mother used to wear, brushes my shoulder.

I open the closet door, coughing fur. The apartment's silent, empty and hot as hell. I tiptoe into the front room. The furniture's heavy, dark, old. I wipe my brow. There's a big black telephone on a polished table, matching green chairs, a carved sideboard, and a sofa filled with feathers. I know this from the sound it makes as I sit down. An exhausted wheeze, as if . . .

'Mama?'

Suddenly I remember a grass soup called Shav she served in the hot weather. I can see her slopping this soup over the thin china bowls she cherished. Soon she'd need an eye operation for a detached retina. All right, maybe it wasn't soup. Maybe it was stewed prunes.

Was Rosalie's somebody's old mother?

There's no ashtrays. No smell of perfume, no tossed-off gold lamé dresses, or high-heeled shoes. No nylons draped over chairs. Who was this Rosalie? The whole place smells like chicken.

Something don't feel right.

I turn on the air-cooling under the window, breaking my rule never to disturb the scene. What I'd like now's an ice cold Schlitz, the beer that made Milwaukee famous. Beer.

Smokes. I decide to leave. Go home, I tell myself. Forget Rosalie. Open a beer. I'm halfway to the door. Then I remember. I dumped the smokes. What's a beer without smokes? I don't have enough money left for beer and smokes. I grab the telephone cord and jerk it free from the wall socket. Before I know what I'm doing, I've trashed the room and mussed my pompadour. I breathe hard. To make up for the loss of my hair, I pour myself two fingers of schnapps from a dusty glass decanter on the sideboard. Leaning crookedly against the wall, I hold the glass in both hands to steady it, and gulp.

What is this stuff? Carbonic acid?

There's a dull ache in the middle of my chest. The schnapps is thick and syrupy, and so strong I can feel it in my armpits.

I lurch to the bedroom, lose my balance and bang my shoulder against the doorframe. In the bedroom, I open and shut a dresser drawer. I find big pants, a photograph of a dog. A mirror above the dresser shines. I take a strangled breath. On top of the dresser, a pair of neatly folded eyeglasses, taped together in one corner and a china bowl. My heart squeezes. I don't want to look in the bedroom closet. Sure enough, it's filled with old dresses on crappy metal hangers. Them old lady shoes.

Then I hear footsteps.

Slowly I move back to the front room. Pistol whipped by the pain in my shoulder and down my left arm from my encounter with the doorframe, I flatten myself against the wall and fumble for my scarf. The footsteps come closer. Closer and closer. Then a figure fills my line of vision. It's Fank in a sharp suit.

'Fank?'

He don't answer.

The room's getting darker at the edges. Darker and hotter. For one crazy moment, scalp prickling, I think maybe the Hypnotiser double booked. I close my eyes and begin to swing the scarf in a lethal arc above my head. Then, swaying slightly, I slide slowly down the wall.

Georgi Gospodinov

Cherry Tea

Translated by Kalina Filipova

On the day he would receive that extraordinary sign, he was hurrying along his usual route. It is important to add here that his purposeful air was more a matter of habit than necessity. A peculiar kind of alibi. He looked like someone who had pressing tasks and urgent meetings to attend: he kept anxiously glancing at his watch and quickening his pace. The destination of this resolutely brisk walking was always the same: a little tobacconist shop. He'd deliberately chosen one which was several blocks away from where he lived. There were at least three reasons for his choice: it was just the right distance for a slightly longer walk, it opened earlier than any other tobacconist around and, besides, there was something in the smile of the young woman who ran it that was that little bit more than just ordinary politeness. Or at least it seemed so to him. He'd take his cigarettes, smile absently and then head back with the same urgency. Not that anyone was expecting him anywhere. More than six months ago he'd quit his job as an editor in order to devote himself completely to his own writing. Some time ago his first book of short stories had caused quite a stir, at least as far as these things went around here, and this had given him the courage to ditch the drudgery of reading other people's manuscripts and dedicate more time to his talent. He shut himself at home, stopped seeing anyone on business, then stopped seeing anyone for pleasure, either. And – nothing. He hadn't published a single sentence for six months. Gradually even the periodicals stopped pestering him for contributions and gave up on him. And even now he was filled with a vague feeling of guilt and a sense of failure which made him increase his pace as though there was a story on his computer waiting to be finished.

Later he would remember clearly how that particular day something made him stop beside the phone box at the corner, which he always passed by. There was something scribbled in black on its grimy glass side-panel. He went up closer and read it: '*When I married, I became an old woman*'. He liked it: it could be a good opening line for a story, he thought, something his muse, who'd lately completely abandoned him, had graciously sent him. He immediately took out his little notebook to copy the sentence and it was only then that he noticed there was also a phone number. He read it over several times to make sure he wasn't mistaken. He wasn't. It was his number. Still, just to be sure, he copied it into his notebook. He felt stupid but picked up the phone and dialled his own number, as if half expecting to hear his voice answer at the other end. But there was only the ringing tone. He stood, hypnotised by the sound, for about a minute, then hung up slowly and came out of the phone box. On that early April morning the street was quite deserted, except for the lady with the lapdog (a white Pomeranian) who was just turning the corner and the delivery van which was unloading bread in front of the corner shop at the far end of the street. Nothing very suspicious, really. He took out his handkerchief and quickly wiped the phone number off the glass. It came off more easily than could be expected. He decided not to bother with the sentence itself and headed home. He looked back several times, without really knowing what he expected to see. It crossed his mind to hide in the entrance of one of the apartment blocks, in the hope the perpetrator of the joke might return to the scene of the crime, but then he decided that wouldn't be a very good idea, or in very good taste: it reminded him of the kind of crap he used to read over the years as an editor. He would go home instead and calmly think things over.

He sat down, opened his notebook, lit a cigarette and started thinking of all the various possibilities. His mind was working fast, faster than at any time in the last six months. He kept reading the sentence over and over again, scribbling words, connecting them with arrows, then crossing them out and starting over again. He felt a peculiar sort of pleasure: after all, he was working again – writing, inventing. He'd come up with three different theories, each as bizarre as the next.

The darkest one was that he'd flipped his lid completely and had developed some weird sort of somnambulism or lunacy (which sounded better), as a result of which he would get up at night, unlock the front door, go out and write strange sentences on phone boxes, signing them with his own phone number. True, the handwriting wasn't his but then, with some forms of schizophrenia, this could happen.

The second theory involved his ex-wife: perhaps she'd suddenly remembered him, had come back from Florida where she was living happily with her new husband and, consumed by some hidden rancour, come up with that perfidious plan just to get back at him. All of which struck him as even more implausible than his first theory.

The third had as its main character a failed writer whose manuscript he'd rejected sometime in the past. And now, day after day, sentence by sentence, the whole manuscript would be published on the glass side panel of the phone box. And every time there'd also be the phone number of the guilty editor – for the whole world to see: every time some passer-by read those wonderful, underrated sentences, they would ring the number to thank the author for them, but would in fact stab the conscience of the cold-hearted editor.

No, no – that's just too silly, he thought to himself, after re-reading all three versions. But then, you had to admit his imagination had suddenly gone wild – for the first time in ages. He felt exhausted and slept as he hadn't slept in half a year.

On the following morning he woke up filled with a pleasant foreboding that something was about to happen. The small cherry orchard behind the block of flats (three trees, to be precise) had blossomed overnight. The sun was shining, there were sparrows flitting from branch to branch in the tree below his window, and all this made yesterday's story seem somewhat brighter and slightly unreal. He set off along his usual route to the tobacconist's and the closer he got to the phone box, the more he slowed down. He decided not to stop but instead passed by very slowly. There wasn't anything new written on the glass panel. He felt cheated. There really should have been another sign, another lead of some sort. Someone wasn't playing according to the rules: no sooner had they begun than they stopped. He entered the shop visibly crestfallen and asked for his usual two packs of cigarettes; as he was putting them away the young woman behind the counter said quietly: 'I was asked to give you this,' and she handed him a small envelope.

'How did you know it was for me?' he asked nervously. But glancing at the envelope (which was, horror of horrors, rose-coloured!) he clearly saw his name written on it.

'That's what she said. The woman who . . . She knew you came in every morning . . .' The girl was obviously embarrassed. 'I've read your stories – your book . . . You don't look much like the photo . . .'

'What did she look like, that woman?'

'Well, a bit strange, really. I don't know . . . She never comes in here.'

Unfortunately just then several people entered. Embarrassed, he thanked the girl and left. He clutched the letter in his pocket and decided to wait until he got home before he opened it. But as he was passing by the phone box he had a brainwave and stopped. He took out the envelope for a moment, compared the handwriting on it to that of the sentence on the side of the phone booth and then, looking pleased with himself, went on his way. It was the same hand; the game was going on. Once in his room, he took the letter out. There was only his name on it, no address, and only a post-office box number and the initials R. O. A. as a return address. And why this terrible rose pink, he wondered, as if we're in the nineteenth century? And all those envelopes, and letters? But when he opened the letter all his scorn and superiority evaporated.

At the top of the white sheet of paper he saw the name Rosalie Ossipovna-Aromat. Slowly, he said it out loud.

How could anyone think of such a terrible and absurd name? So that's what the initials stood for. And of course, that explained the colour of the envelope. He sniffed it, but no, it wasn't scented. Or perhaps there was just the faintest trace of an aroma, like a perfume bottle that had been open for more than a century.

Under the name, in the same slightly slanting hand, there were several strange sentences, separated by dots:

. . .

It was such a romantic wedding, and later – what fools! what babies!

. . .

The parlourmaid, Nadya, fell in love with an exterminator of bugs and black beetles.

. . .

They teased the girl with castor oil, and therefore she did not marry.

. . .

In a love letter: Stamp enclosed for reply.

He read them over again and again. He changed their order, added the sentence from the phone box, arranged them in all sorts of different configurations. At one point they began to sound like a story – or the bare outlines of a story, rather, the bare bones, the skeleton of a story. Then he thought they seemed like five different stories, or like five openings of stories, or like five closing lines: they would do equally well, either way. But none of this gave him any important answers. Where had they come from? Who had sent them? Why him? And what on earth was this weird game, which he'd suddenly found himself involved in for two mornings now, supposed to mean?

The sentences sounded vaguely familiar, but he couldn't for the life of him think of where they might be from. Maybe that was the point. He just had to discover their origin. There was something Russian, something classic about them – the combination of the sentimental and the cavalier, the word order, the rose-coloured envelope, even the name of the woman who'd sent it.

He eliminated Dostoevsky first. Not that he wasn't sentimental but there were other things there, other smells and other miasmas . . . Here the aroma was faint, light, with just a touch of irony. He took down Turgenev from the bookshelf and leafed through him impatiently. No, no – no. Gogol – no, there's no way you could mistake that nose. Lermontov: more coldly demonic; besides, he practically knew him by heart. Bunin? . . . He kept on, in no particular order. There was one single one left. Chekhov, of course, dear old Anton Pavlovich. He took down all eight volumes from the top shelf and dusted them carefully, almost caressing the hard covers. The darling.

He slowly leafed through volume after volume, losing himself in them, and the hours passed with a peculiar kind of Chekhovian ease. There was something healing, elating about his reading, as if the three cherry trees from the little back garden had transplanted themselves into his living room: the wooden floor creaked gently and pink blossoms drifted down onto the pages. But Rosalie Ossipovna just refused to appear. The room was like a provincial railway station on a Sunday, swarming with all kinds of Mashas, Olgas, Dunyashas, Sonechkas, Anna Sergeevnas and Vera

Yosifovnas passing each other hurriedly . . . But no Rosalie Ossipovna. By dawn he was almost driven to despair and he began to open the covers of each volume and spread them like the wings of a partridge, shaking them as if hoping this strange lady might fall like a light feather from between the pages. Then he started smelling them, sniffing at the pages like a hound, hoping he might at least discover her faint scent. Still nothing. Finally, crestfallen, he reached for the last volume; he had little hope left, since it contained only notes and letters. He opened it at random and his eyes fell directly on the name. Rosalie Ossipovna-Aromat! The woman from the phone box appeared, suddenly grown old after her marriage. What fools! What babies! And everything – everything. The heading read 'From Chekhov's Notebooks'. He'd never paid it much attention before. The mysterious Rosalie Ossipovna was either some barmy Chekhov fan who, for some obscure reason, wanted *him* to finish those unwritten stories (in which case he was being given a commission), or she simply wanted to make a gift of them to him, to help him get out of the deep hole he was in. Or, most likely, it was a bit of both. In any case, it was the nicest thing anyone had done for him lately. Finely crafted, with all those signs and mysteries.

That very minute he took out a white sheet of paper and wrote:

Dear Rosalie Ossipovna,

As I write to you, there are three cherry trees blossoming in my living room, the floor is covered with rosy petals and a glorious April dawn is breaking outside. In short:

spring, with all its details, in the word of our mutual –.
Forgive me, I cannot find the right word; or I'm afraid
to say it out loud, rather.

I feel, dear Rosalie Ossipovna, profoundly confused.
Pray, tell me honestly: do we know each other – and why
are you doing all this for me? I just do not know what
to say . . .

I just – Lord, all those repetitions . . . I beg you, give
me a sign, write to me, perhaps we could have some tea
sometime.

Yours,
N. N.

He got up, put the letter in an envelope and went out. For
the first time in ages he took a different route.

Two days later, just as he was on his way out to the tobacconist's, he saw a rose-coloured envelope in his letterbox. He
opened it immediately and, as he was rushing back up the
stairs, he read:

Dear N. N.,

I am pleased, indeed content . . . I just wanted to give
you a sign. Your unwritten stories are as missed as those
of our mutual – let us say inventor, or inspiration – it
matters not what we call him. You will understand, of
course, that I must disappear; I could be going away,
if you like, to Yalta with my husband (his rheumatism
gets worse in the spring) . . . I shall look forward to your
stories.

*One last thing: don't put off drinking the tea we
shan't have together. It's growing cold.*

Yours,
Rosalie Ossipovna

Perhaps she was the very Rosalie Ossipovna-Aromat of the
notebooks. Who knows: perhaps all this was a muffled cry,
the desire to be born in someone's story, the gentle plea of
someone who is only a name. The name of Rosalie, he smiled
to himself. All we have left is the name, as that professor from
Bologna had written. But that's just rhetoric, really. In fact,
all we have is the story. Somewhere a woman was waiting to
be invented. And he would drink all the tea in the world with
her.

It was then that he turned the sheet over and saw the post-
script:

*P.S. By the way, have you noticed the tobacconist also sells
all kinds of teas – even cherry tea. And someone expects
you there, every day . . .*

Mechanically, he reached for a cigarette. But he'd run out
of cigarettes. How could he be such a fool! While he ran
towards the little tobacconist shop the day took shape all by
itself, with a peculiarly Chekhovian ease. They would have
some tea. And then he would write.

Ali Smith

Trachtenbauer

A tiny little schoolboy with the name of Trachtenbauer was
at my door when I opened it.

I say tiny little and that's literally what I mean. He was
about eight inches tall, the size of a sizeable penis, the average
height of a cat, which meant that when the doorbell rang
while I was pouring my cornflakes into the bowl and I went
through to the hall thinking it would be the postman and
opened the door and looked out, it was as if there was no one
there at all, and it was only as I was about to close it that I
heard the squeaking of a small voice at shin level.

Hello! he squeaked. I am Trachtenbauer.

I looked down.

Grey cap, little red shield on the front; grey, blue-and-red-
striped blazer, little red shield on the top pocket; white shirt,
top button buttoned at the collar; tight knotted blue-and-
red-striped school tie tucked into grey pullover; grey shorts;
grey knee socks; perfectly-tailored diminutive leather brogues
as if created, designed and sewn by tiny hands in the leathery
sweatshop of an imagination like Enid Blyton's.

How did you reach the doorbell? I said.

Maths, of course, he squeaked. I simply calculated the exact
angle and square-metred area of your front doorstep and
drive and the exact angle at which to stand to find the closest

angle of elevation from which to launch a small missile, i.e. a pebble from your driveway. I am top at maths. I am naturally brilliant at many things and it helps that most of my talents have been nurtured by excellent schooling and supremely good parenting. And I'm here today to tell you that all of these things are available to everybody in this country, rich or poor, who works hard and plays fair, and that we're jolly lucky to be living at such a lucky and civilised time, don't you agree?

Eh, I suppose so, I said.

The tiny little schoolboy glowed at my feet as if he'd just won a debating trophy.

A digression: you may at this still quite early stage in the story be feeling cheated and annoyed, if you are a person, like me, who likes your short stories to be about real things in the real world. You may be feeling frustrated, too, if what you like in fiction is – and what you expected of me tonight was – the kind of story where, for instance, what people have for breakfast, how they spoon it from bowl to mouth or scrape whatever they take on their toast onto their toast, reveals not just their characters but their whole lives, held there in one perfectly pitched moment. How their slightest movements round the wood or Formica tables in their kitchens, how the way they brush their teeth before they leave for work in the mornings, reveal the emotional richnesses and gains and losses of their lives.

I understand. Here's some contemporary verisimilitude. A woman is standing blindfolded in a communal cell in Abu Ghraib and her dead brother's body is brought and dumped at her feet. She doesn't know for sure if it's her brother, but that's what they shouted in English when they dumped him:

here's your brother. Her sister is standing in the same cell. She is also blindfolded. The woman crouches, puts her tied hands down and feels a slick of something warm on the body. Is it blood? She doesn't know. She can't see. She raises her hands to her nose. It smells like blood. She stands up again. It's difficult to stand up when you're blindfolded and your hands are tied. She senses her sister kneeling down now. She says to her sister: Is he breathing? Her sister answers, but only after several minutes.

No.

So, back here in the UK, I opened my door and at my feet was an eight-inch-high perfect representation of a public schoolboy.

Not representation, he squeaked. I'm not a representation. I'm the real thing.

What did you say your name was? I said.

Trachtenbauer, he said. Trachtenbauer. Trachtenbauer. Trachtenbauer. It's an old English family name.

It sounds a bit German to me, I said.

Yes, he said. To the uninitiated ear it would sound German. But the original Trachtenbauers are listed in the Domesday Book. I am not lying. I never lie. I cannot tell a lie. I'd never lie to you. I do however have interesting fun in my advanced German class with the many hilarious random things my name could be translated to mean, were it by any stretch of the imagination a name that wasn't wholly English. For example: Farmer of costumes. Costumed cage. Endeavouring farmer. Cage of striving. Dressed-up cage. Endeavouring cage. Endeavouring pawn. Dressed-up pawn.

Dressed-up porn? I said.

Pawn, he squeaked. As in chessboard, lowest ranking

piece. Pawn. Pawn.

To my amazement, he went completely red with anger. He was waving his minute fists in the air. He was stamping his tiny feet on my doorstep and squeaking the word 'pawn' over and over. It really did sound like porn; well, upper-middle-class porn.

I closed the front door. I'd had enough of him, frankly. He was hysterical. I didn't want a hysterical public schoolboy, even that small a one, in my house.

To tell you the truth, I didn't really want to have to be taking part in this kind of story either. It's not the kind of story I'd have chosen, myself. I'd have preferred something much more utilitarian and social. I went, when I was a schoolgirl, to one of the first Scottish comprehensives. This was, oh, years and years before nine-eleven. Of course, the world's completely changed now, as we all know. Nothing can possibly be the same again. I remember, from those old gone days, the feeling of being sixteen and knowing I could say, Nuclear power, no thanks. I had the leaflets. I wore the badge. My father nodded. He said, That's how change happens, girl; that's how history happens, through people like you questioning the status quo.

My father, by the way, is a brilliant man, now in his eighties, who had to leave school in his early teens because his mother needed him to earn money, after his own father, who'd been gassed in the First World War, died. He worked as an electrician all his life. He and my mother put all five of us, me and my four siblings, through a tertiary education that they never even had the dream of having. Both of them were clever. Neither of them was still at school past the age of thirteen. When my father was nineteen he saw, over the side of a Royal Navy cruiser on its way to Malta, forty American soldiers who'd been wrongly parachuted in and had landed miles out in the Mediterranean, and they were calling to each passing ship in the convoy to stop for them and pick them up. When he saw them waving in the water, trying to keep their heads above the wake, and he knew that no ship was ever going to stop for them, that was his education.

As to his children's education, I can see him sitting in his chair by the electric fire and tapping the arm of it with his finger. Because when that war was over, the good thing that came of it, he believed, was that everyone knew that the sons of the poor and the ordinary were equal to the sons of the rich, equally able to go to Eton, to Oxford, to Cambridge – maybe even if they happened to be daughters.

So when I was a schoolgirl, at the height of comprehensive education, we once spent an evening in the same building as the boys and girls of Gordonstoun, school of the royals, at a schools'-night performance of *Macbeth* at the theatre in Inverness, which is where I grew up. It was 1978 or 9, the year of punk, so we had what you might call a common language. After that performance there was a lot of giving each other the finger through the bus windows in the car park of the theatre, and remembering this now makes me think of my sister Anne's trick when she was a schoolgirl ten years earlier than me, whenever her school hockey team was playing a team from a private school, of dribbling effortlessly past public schoolgirl after public schoolgirl simply by saying as she approached with the ball on her stick, Excuse me, Excuse me.

But don't go thinking that what I've been telling you is going to transform this uneasy hybrid of fantasy and reality into something resolved in the end by a bit of touching auto-biographical material. Because it won't. Don't be deceived; don't deceive yourself. This is a Trachtenbauer time we live in.

So I closed the font door on him and went through to the kitchen to have my breakfast, and there he was, Trachten-bauer, standing in the middle of the room, enthusiastic as anything.

Hello again! he said. He was bright as a button.

Actually I quite liked his enthusiasm. It would have been hard not to. It was very endearing.

The Mediterranean, he said, is the inland sea separating Europe from North Africa with Asia to the east. Its surface comprises 2,966,000 square kilometres.

Thanks for that, I said. Useful. And how did you get in here, again?

Simple, he said. Cat-flap. It is a magnet-protected cat-flap, as you presumably know, since you presumably installed it, but of course being a schoolboy I am never without a magnet.

Ah, I said. Of course.

When your magnet-protected cat-flap clicked open I vaulted in, in a single vault, he said. I wish you could have seen me. It was a particularly good vault. I also happen to be best at sport. I am really glad that there will be a Great British Olympics in 2012. Incidentally, I hope you don't mind me saying so, but you are obese.

I'm not obese! I said. I'm only nine-and-a-half stone!

Like so many of our UK contemporary public, if you only ate a lot less and didn't eat a solid diet of saturated fatty foods like for example chips or crisps, you would feel so much healthier and better and happier, and you too would be able to pass through smaller openings, just like me, he said. But the main thing is, don't worry. There's a helpline. I can give you the number for it.

He looked a little larger than his original eight inches now himself. Maybe I had mis-seen him the first time, but he looked about a foot-and-a-half high. It was as if he was actually growing in stature now that he'd got himself into the house. For example, he was big enough to reach and pick up a knife off the table, which he was doing now, examining it to see what it was made of. He put it down again. He nodded to himself as if confirming something. He looked all round my kitchen and nodded some more.

Cornflakes, he said approvingly, and nodded.

Look, I said. I'm very busy. What is it you actually want?

I don't want anything, he said. You want me. I'm your free government initiative.

Initiative for what? I said.

For initiative, Trachtenbauer said. I am soon to be issued free to all households. Congratulations. You've been selected as a test household. Soon everyone will have me, or be able to phone a freephone number and get extra copies of me, even copies in Urdu and Bengali and French and Chinese and Welsh and Arabic and Punjabi for people who happen not to speak English well enough for the English version of me.

You mean, there's more than one of you? I said.

I am unique, but soon to be made available to millions, he said.

But what if I don't want to be a test household? I said. What if I don't want you?

Don't want me? Trachtenbauer said.

He laughed as if he couldn't imagine anything more ridiculous.

I am invaluable, he said. You'll see. I've already made things so much better for you since I entered your house.

How? I said.

The value of your property will have risen notably since I arrived, he said. You get a better mortgage with a Trachtenbauer.

Look, Trachtenberger, I said –

Bauer, he said. You can trust a Trachten*bauer*.

Yes, Trachten*bauer*, I said. But don't you have a first name I could call you? Trachtenbauer feels a bit, well, unwieldy.

I do, but I'm afraid I'm not permitted to tell you it, he said.

Why not? I said.

Our focus groups have decided that it's better if I'm called Trachtenbauer so that there's just a small something lingering at the back of your-the-consumer's mind to remind you of the last world war. Remember? When Britain was right? When Britain was victorious? he said.

Look, I said. This is private property. I'm asking you politely to leave.

I'm afraid this boy just can't do that, mate, he squeaked. This boy's your friend. This boy's here to stay. This boy'd never run out on you. This boy stood on the burning deck whence all but he had fled.

What? I said.

The boy stood on the burning deck whence all but he had fled, he said. *The flame that lit the battle's wreck shone round him o'er the dead. Yet beautiful and bright he stood, as born to rule the storm; a creature of heroic blood, a proud, though child-like form*. It's a poem by Mrs Felicia Hemans, a lady writer. Would you like to hear my Gang Show song? It's a jolly good one. I could teach you the words. It's not difficult. Even quite slow people can remember them.

No, I said. Look, I'm going upstairs. I'll be down in ten minutes. And if you're not gone from here by the time I get downstairs, I'm calling the police.

It's you they'd arrest, though, not me, Trachtenbauer said.

Why? I said. Why would anyone arrest me? I haven't done anything wrong.

Trachtenbauer shrugged. He gave me a burning look. He put his schoolbag on the floor and leaned one arm on a tiny hipbone.

You've been warned, I said.

You've been warned, he squeaked back. They'll keep you in prison for as long as they like, too.

I couldn't believe the schoolboy cheek of it.

I went upstairs into the bathroom and put toothpaste on my toothbrush and I knew as soon as I looked in the mirror and saw myself there unchanged, same as ever, that I'd simply been hallucinating.

I bet you're relieved to hear it. I bet you're relieved this story is finally back on track.

I looked at myself in the mirror and I wondered if I'd maybe been drinking the night before and had simply forgotten how drunk I'd been. I wondered if I'd ingested a drug that had made me hallucinate. Because there was no way on earth, no way in any trustworthy verisimilitude, that a small pert schoolboy a foot and a half high had got into my house.

No.

It was as ridiculous to think this as it was to imagine that anyone, never mind a tiny little schoolboy with the name of Trachtenbauer, had just told me that the police could, for instance, arrest me, an innocent person, and hold me indefinitely without charge. Nobody could do that to the law. I lived in the kind of country where, just like short stories were short stories and behaved appropriately, the law was the law and was there to protect people from this kind of thing. It was every bit as mad to imagine such a travesty as it was to conjure up a tiny little schoolboy who came preaching into my life through the cat-flap; as insane as it would be if I were to look out of the bathroom window now, look up into the sky and see that the sky itself was shrouded, the whole real world tented over with a massive expanse, an enormous blazered Trachtenbauer so huge that he hid the sky, so that not just my house, not just my street, but the whole town, maybe the whole country, was the plaything of a giant schoolboy who, when he leaned in with his huge hand, a hand as big as five good arable fields, bigger than five football pitches, and moved something from one area of his model village to another, he knocked a small copse of trees down and wrecked a busy traffic junction and tore up the foundations of three adjoining streets as he did, by mistake, because it would be impossible not to have some innocent casualties if your hands were so big and what you were dealing with was so small.

No.

I opened the bathroom window and leaned out. The world looked the same. Everything was happening as it usually did on a weekday morning. There were people walking up and down the street. There were people going back and fore in cars. There were leaves shifting in the wind on the trees and birds singing in the gardens. There were small fluffed clouds in a bright blue sky.

I brushed my teeth.

But when I came downstairs again I found the cat cowering in a corner of the hall licking a bleeding gash in her leg.

Trachtenbauer, who now seemed somehow larger, nearly the size of a normal ten-year-old child, was sitting cross-legged on the carpet in my front room folding the pages he was ripping out of my Penguin Classics copy of Robert Tressell's *The Ragged Trousered Philanthropists* into origami swans.

What are you doing to my book? I shouted.

Top at origami, he squeaked in a squeak that was a little noticeably deeper than his previous squeaks. *Animal Farm* next. Have you any other outdated books you won't be needing any more? Don't think much of your taste, I'm afraid. No Biggles. No *Just So Stories*. No Harry Potter.

Trachtenbauer, did you just hurt my cat? I said.

Your cat attacked me, he squeaked. It's a terrorist.

He brandished a pair of bloodied eyebrow tweezers in the air.

Did you stab my cat with those tweezers? I said.

See how dangerous tweezers are? he deep-squeaked.

He waved their ends at me like little antennae.

Right, I said. That's it. I'm off out. And when I come back I'll have two Alsatians with me, and believe me, they won't be scared of tweezers.

I pulled on my coat. He scuttled across the room sending origami swans flying and stood between me and the front door with his arms flung out wide.

You mustn't go out without being prepared, he said.

Prepared for what? I said.

An emergency, he said. It could happen at any time. Do you know where and how to turn off the water, gas and electricity supplies?

But he was now definitely taller than he'd been when I'd opened the door to him. He was about four feet tall, and growing, and I saw for the first time that under the too-small school cap, rather than the clear face of a boy he had the strangely wizened, strangely shrunken face of a man in his late forties or early fifties.

Keep calm, he shouted. Nothing to worry about. Go in. Stay in. Tune in. Local radio will keep you informed. Whatever you do, don't panic.

He smiled as he blocked my doorway. I had to get past him. What could I do?

Excuse me, I said.

The old ones work every time. He stepped to the side without thinking. I slipped past him and out through the door into the front garden, fast as I could go down the path. When I turned back I saw him in my doorway. His buttons were bulging now across his chest. His shorts were strained at their seams. As I watched, his stripy blazer ripped in two. It hung off both his arms like ragged Union Jacks.

Trachtenbauer, I shouted from the gate. You're getting . . . so big.

He nodded, he was all enthusiasm; I saw him swelling and swelling, taller and wider; he was much bigger than me now, and now he was as high as my downstairs rooms, and now he jutted a shoulder under the doorframe of the front door and broke it, effortlessly, shattering the bricks and plaster of my house, it had taken him only a few seconds to; and when he spoke his voice broke too, it rumbled out of him like a tank.

I'm coming of age, he said.

David Means

The Gulch

The cross was jury-rigged out of pressure-treated wood ties, the kind used for gardening, as boarders on raised beds, and for retaining walls, secured at the cross point – for lack of a better phrase – with a hitch of cotton rope, ashen in colour from exposure to the elements, stolen from Mrs Highsmith's yard; a clothesline that had for several years held the garments of Rudy Highsmith (involved). Fingering it in the evidence room, Detective Collard could feel the droopy sway of a line laden with wet garments, and he could easily imagine Rudy's ragged jeans, holes shredded white, pale blue and growing lighter under the warmth of the sun, picking up the breeze on some late-summer afternoon, while a dog barked rhapsodically along the edge of the woods. The Highsmith house was on the outskirts of Bay City, Michigan, not far from the gulch, and was known – to a few locals, at least – as the house with laundry on the line, one last holdout of the air-drying tradition. The cross was set in a hole that had been dug by a fold-up trench shovel. (This was admitted by Ron Bycroff, age seventeen, the oldest in the bunch. Bycroff openly confessed – after five hours of interrogation – to digging the hole and securing the cross and arranging the ropes and so on, but not to the actual pounding of the spikes, or even to being there at that point. (He was there, he later admitted to his lawyer, but not in spirit and heart, and he had his eyes turned away most of the time. I just couldn't look. I heard the sounds and that was enough.) During the trial, this confession was thrown out by Judge Richards because it had been obtained by coercion – veiled threats (You'd have to be ashamed, boy, you'd have to be as deeply ashamed as anyone on this good earth, doing what you did, boy. How'd you feel if I took you down there to the gulch myself, right now, to take a little look around? I might just take you down there tonight). On the other hand, the trench shovel was from the Bycroff's garage. During his interrogation, Detective Collard was unable to remove from his mind's eye (is there a better phrase?) the impressive vision of the spikes in the victim's palms, deep, dimpling the skin. The small hand and the blood around the entry point in the beam of his flashlight had given him a sense of the softness of human flesh and the vulnerability of hands to piercing implements. The skin on the victim's hands – he knew because he reached out and touched one – was soft and smooth, like a chamois or the inside of a dog's ear.

For his part, Rudy Highsmith lay out the details of the murder between snot-filled snorts, divulging the story in breathy gushes. The whole thing was Al Stanton's idea, he said. He came up with it. Like he was preaching to us. He was saying this weird shit about how it was time to open up the cosmos. He told us Sammy was the perfect age and all, sixteen and a half, and that it would be good for him to rise from the dead. It was all his idea, honest. He came up with it first. This claim that Stanton was the one who dreamed up the scheme (for lack of a better word) seemed dubious to Detective Collard. The hefty, moonfaced kid – a linebacker on the high-school team – seemed dense in thought, a bit slow on the uptake but also openly sweet and likable. His eyes contained a sadness that came – Collard knew – from the fact that his father had disappeared when he was eight, taking off in his bass boat onto Lake Erie. (The most likely scenario was that he drove his boat down to Cleveland, sold it, and headed to Florida to find a new way of life.) His mother, a heavy drinker and prone to violence, showed up every few months on police blotter as a DWI and eventually became known around the station as an SAWTH, a Serious Accident Waiting To Happen. There were – any policeman could tell you – those who were preordained to fiery deaths, those most certain to be found frozen in a ditch outside of town, those whose future lay out there like a wide-open bear trap, ready to snap shut when the right amount of pressure was applied on the right spot. Stanton's mother was one of them.

(Dead faces, Collard thought, often spoke to the world, sending out final messages that were surprisingly heartfelt and concise. Dead lovers wore the betrayed smirks of the heartbroken. Dead adulterers had a worried cast to their mouths. The murdered had the silent look of the betrayed, glancing to one side or the other to indicate the direction of the perpetrator's flight. The tortured held their lips as wide as possible at the arrogance of the living, wanting above all to arrange for a conversation with the future, to let the world know what was what. But the victim in the crime down in the gulch seemed to say something else. His face was resigned and silent and non-assuming. (Collard was fully aware that it was easy to see something that wasn't there, just as some drifter had found the Virgin Mary under a viaduct in Detroit last winter, spotting her face in a splotch of salt and snow splatter cast up against the cement pylon by the passing snow ploughs.))

Collard (who was big on fishing) had a theory that the truth always sat deep, waiting to be snagged by a verbal grappling hook and lugged to the surface. With the boys in this case, he would later think, his technique had been off. He had given his cards away. His voice had cracked, his words arrived unstable. The boy (Stanton) was not exactly cocky. But he was unusually sure-footed and assured when he said that he had nothing to do with the crime, that he had stood to the side while the other kids performed the rites; he had done nothing except pass, at one point, the spikes over to Bycroff, who held them while someone else, maybe Highsmith, maybe not, because he wasn't really looking, pounded them in with the croquet hammer.

Bycroff blamed Stanton who, in turn, blamed Highsmith, who went around himself to blame Bycroff in what most detectives traditionally call the golden hoop of blame. This three-way tag of blame seemed particularly fine to Collard, who had gone so far as to hold the actual gag bandana up in Rudy Highsmith's face. A green snot-stiff cloth that unknotted and straightened still seemed to hold some residue of the victim's last words.

It was impossible to imagine such pain without inflicting some on yourself, Collard thought, and listening to descriptions of the event during the trial, he bit his nails to the quick just to find some small amount of pain from which to extrapolate the rest. Most in the courtroom did something to this affect. The jury box was stuffed with nail chewers. Lawyers snapped their fingers under the clamp of their clipboard, and reporters in the gallery dug their fingers into their arms, pinching hard, as if to check their consciousness. Most imagined the suffering as a dreary succumbing to the knowledge of the pain, an almost delirious unknowing state as the nails came through – the first bloom of pain, and then a feeling of being fixed there, yielding to something soft and – at least the way Collard imagined it, still thinking in terms of the laundry on those lines – fluffy and starch-smelling. By the time the third spike was pounded in the boy was safely afloat on his own emergency juices! What did it mean, some of the jury wondered, to lay claim to the idea that the boy was not suffering as much as one thought? In an attempt to lighten the immensity of the crime, a pain expert was brought in to testify that the body did have certain chemicals that came to the defence of the inflicted in this kind of situation. (Torture, on the other hand, was a matter of countering the body's natural opiates, of inducing pain incrementally, with a finesse that worked around these chemical defences.) The boys, in their quick, careless plunge into the deepest heart of whatever it was, darkness or evil (the prosecution couldn't exactly decide), had nailed the boy to the cross hard and fast, producing a flush of pain that had quickly produced a flood of endorphins. Shock was nothing but the deepest joke on consciousnes, and when this boy, on that cold fall night, was faced with spikes – through his hands and legs, as he twisted up against the face of the jury-rigged cross – he flew the coop, so to speak, and became nothing but a vapor of soul-stuff who just so happened to inhabit a body that was, at that moment, being crucified. (The defence argued.)

If anyone had to confront the issue at hand it was the coroner, Samuel Bracket. Bay City seemed to produce a disproportionate number of accidental full-body piercings. Boys fell onto implements, impaled themselves through playful jousting. The coroner took care to avoid an inclination he had to find pleasure in the absurd foibles of those who lay on the slabs for examination; he tried the best he could to push away the amusement he found in absurd deaths, caused by foolish actions. Stunts were pulled in the deep heart of night. Attempts were made to defy physical law. Stupidity was like dust, or the earth itself. He drove home that evening – after the examination of the boy's body, making note of the spike holes, the gash along the mouth, the stress fracture in the wrists; making note of the fact that the boy had died at approximately three in the morning. Driving home, listening to Schubert on the car stereo, he considered the bloodless silence of the boy's open eyes (which he shut), fixed upward, and the paradigmatic (was that the word?) palm holes. The boy's body – slightly glistening, with dimples of fat along the waist – seemed to hold a gentle repose, as if giving in to gravity. (Most of the time, a body, during the first hours after death, seemed to lift away from the surface of the table, barely tethered. A soul-empty body was as light as a seed pod, the brittle shell of a cicada.) Of course his imagination was getting ahead of him. He was seeing what he wanted to see in those eyes, pale and sad, somewhat elegaic, dark grey with a bit of blue around the senseless dilation of the pupils. On the way home – glancing over at the dreary waters of the Saginaw River – his thoughts ranged from puncture wounds, to tetanus, and then landed naturally upon the one time he had been impaled: this was in a town called Brandford, near New Haven, Connecticut, goofing around with his buddies, walking barefoot along a break wall of cemented boulders, enjoying the sense of being surefooted against the wind gusts, which were coming hard in off Long Island Sound that morning, when he felt something impinge upon his foot. A strange tingling sensation. Nothing painful until he looked down and saw the point protruding near his toes. Then he became aware of a numb pain, remote and far off. He began running in panic, the board flopping like a wooden clog while his friends laughed and taunted him until it became clear to them what exactly was going on: he had gone into that realm which few kids entered, but which they all thought about. He had stepped on the proverbial nail. (You'll get a nail through your foot if you walk barefoot.) (In the car he tried to make sense of the physics of the accident, calculating the amount of force it would take to send a nail all the way through his foot, adding to the formula the fact that he had been stepping hard on the rocks at the time, doing a jaunty balancing act for his friends, until the nail sank in near the forefoot, up far enough to allow it to slide between the metatarsal bones.) What he could remember more than anything was the odd sense of reorientation the nail had given him until one kid yanked it out while another held his foot, and he, in turn, unleashed a high seagull scream that, in turn, sent the real gulls sweeping up from the beach into the sky.

None of the boys attended a church or had any formal religious education. All three devoted their spiritual energies to killing time, going up to the beach to smoke hash, or over to Detroit to smuggle beer across the bridge from Canada, loading it up by the case and transporting it past the unsuspecting border guards. Into the gap these facts formed, folks inserted wedges of philosophical thought and tried to avoid the possibility that the reenactment of a two-thousand-year-old event was pure senselessness on the part of teenagers who in no way meant to crack the universal fabric apart or to urge a messianic event onto the world. One commentator on a cable news channel argued that it was important to consider the possibility that these boys, in what was certainly a scattershot approach, were trying to find a last ditch way into grace. Good boys from good families had dragged the victim – there was a double-rut line of heel marks from the main road down into the gulch – to the spot under a clear, star-filled late fall sky, erected a cross, dug a hole with a fold-up entrenchment tool, without really thinking. (One professor at the University of Michigan made a connection between the trench shovel, the poetry of Wilfred Owen and the Great War. The soil in Michigan – glacial gravel in the gulch, with remnants of Lake Erie bed fossils – was close in consistency to the bottom of the trenches at Verdun. Another professor, hearing the story reported on the nightly news, brought forth Walter Benjamin's theory of a messianic cessation of happening. He tried to draw (with shaky logic) a parallel between the mock event, the young ruffians (his words) putting their friend up on the cross, working at some subconscious level, and Benjamin's concept of a 'revolutionary chance in the fight for the oppressed past'. The deep impulse these kids had was to begin a conversation with the universe, as it is known, and the unknown, hidden part that can only be seen when you rend the fabric of time/space, he said, throwing his arms wide open before the class and then, composing himself, laying his hands flat on the desk, staying like that for a moment until – as was his habit – he reached up to adjust the dimple of his tie, pulling it tight to his throat. The students, who were used to these sudden outbursts, sat back in their chairs and glanced at each other knowingly. They were close in age to the kids in the gulch and found it hard to imagine that the fuck-ups, probably stoned out of their minds on PCP, or crystal meth, had anything other than simple time-killing intentions in mind.)

For her part, Emma Albee, an English teacher at Bay City High School, felt duty bound to talk about the event in the gulch. (A team of trauma control agents had been sent to help those students who were suffering changes in behavior due to the death of their friend (although in truth he had no friends, and was for the most part a loner who had, before his death, secured the wrath of most of his schoolmates).) She spoke carefully to the class, saying, yes, the action of the three boys was evil, in that they were free not to crucify their friend, just as you are free to do something or not to do something. Her students sat, for once, listening with rapt attention. You see the tragedy of their action, she said, was in the fact that they made a gross error of judgement. We all think about doing things like this, don't we, students? We all have these strange ideas and sometimes we're with our friends and we feel pressured to do them but we do not because we are free, she said, looking for a way into the Camus novel they had just read.

(Several news accounts made a great deal of the fact that the dead boy's face had been excised from several school yearbooks, cut neatly out with razor blades, removed from the grid. Even Detective Collard had smirked at the kid's image: flyaway hair pasted to a pimply brow; a mouth locked into a grimace, caught off guard by the tired school photographer.

(One professor noted a striking resemblence between the victim's face and that of Edgar Allan Poe. The same lean jawbone. The same uncomfortable arrangement between his neck and his lower torso, a general disagreement therein, so that even though he was wearing a striped polo shirt, he still had the bearing of a man in a high clerical collar.))

We just felt like doing it, was Bycroff's statement during his confession. We was just trying it out, you know, like maybe he'd rise again and maybe not but it was worth a shot because he was such a lightweight in this life. Bycroff had been rejected by a series of foster homes that took him around the state of Michigan in the rough shape of a palm, from Kalamazoo upward to Petoskey and then a series of towns on the way back down to Flint. He proved himself deeply incompatible with several domestic situations until at last he found himself under the care of Howard Wood, a surly loner who, most thought, was abusive. We just figured we'd give it a try, he said, working his tongue around his teeth, staring up at Collard, who was listening carefully, tapping his notepad with the eraser side of his pencil. He listened and made notes but knew that this boy's confession would be thrown out of court on some technicality. It was a fast-spoken confession. It came too easily. It was too casual and too offhand to stick. The boy was speaking out of unrelated pains. It was the deeply innocent who often came up with the most honest and realistic confessions of crimes. When they had everything to lose they often threw themselves into it beautifully, like a cliff diver, or was it a pearl diver? Those native boys who found it within themselves to go into the dark waters, their legs kicking up towards the light, flapping softly, their arms extended as they clutched and grabbed. That was the nature of being a detective in these situations; you had to go as deep as you could with the air in your lungs burning and burning and your arms fully extended in the hope that you might bring a pearl to the surface.

He had faced this dead end before in other cases, the sense that one witness would blame the other and then the other *ad infinitum*; the sense that one way or another the criminality would be smeared into something impossibly dull, and that in the end, when the boys were sentenced and when justice was meted out, there would still be unresolved questions of the case that would linger for the rest of his life. There was no end to it. There was no way to turn the story around. He left Bycroff back in the interrogation room, behind the one-way glass, sitting at a wooden table with his chin in his hands. He left him there and went outside to get some sunlight on his face. He stood in the doorway and thought about it. He'd be a retired cop living up north, enjoying the solitude and silence. He'd be fishing on the middle brance of the AuSable one day, casting a muddler into the stream, enjoying the day, and then he'd think of the gulch case and it would all come back to him and he'd remember storming out of the interrogation room into this bright, clear, beautiful light of a fall day in Bay City; he'd cast again into a riffle, thinking about the fish while, at the same time, trying to tweeze apart the facts of the case, remembering the voids, the gaping space between the statements and his failure to get the story straight. He'd spend the rest of the day in the river, or resting on the shore, until his creel was damp and heavy with trout. He'd lift the lid and look in and see the ferns paced around their flanks and their beautiful stripes. Then he'd stand there along the river and feel something else. He was sure of that. By the time he was retired he'd be full of lore, full of the wisdom of a small-town detective who had seen all he could see, acted as witness to the weird manifestations of the human spirit, and he'd have a knowing sense that the best way to cope with the darkness of the world was to concentrate on trying flies, on clamping the hook and spinning the feathers taut with silk thread. The incident at the gulch would be the case that stood out from the others; it would be the classic, the one he pulled out of his hat when the conversations were boring, playing gin rummy or bridge; he'd pull the gulch out and present it as an example of how truly dark the times had become and how out of hand the situation had become; he'd pull it out as an example of the limits of detective work. Every cop had one such case, the true zinger, the one Polaris around which the others rotated, and he'd remember it clearly, not so much the facts around it, the words, the talk, the boys' attitudes and posturing, their attempts to work around the guilt, but mainly the place itself, silent and gritty, with condoms curled like snake skins in the weeds and the ash craters and the used needles, glinting in the moonlight, and how he went up there by himself over the course of the years, late in the night just before dawn, to shoot his sidearm into the air, taking aim at the cup of the Big Dipper, just plugging away at it like that, not because he was feeling helpless, or that the gulch itself inspired him to fire his gun, but because it was a pleasurable thing to do. He thought about this, standing outside the station house taking in the sun. Nothing had changed in Bay City since the incident in the gulch. The media came, set up their dishes, sent the story to the world, got it moving around from head to head, and then just as quickly packed up and left it to be forgotten. On the stream at least he'd have the mercy of forgetfulness and the distance of retrospect and time; everything would be faded and somewhat obscure, except for the facts that he remembered, and he'd go back to his casting, he thought outside the police station, and he'd find mercy in the failings of his memory, and he'd let the case go like that, feeling his line curling around itself behind him as it swung forward, tapering out the toss of his rod, aligning itself along the point of the tip before unleashing smoothly onto the water until the leader, invisible to the fish, guided the fly to a landing at the intended spot. But for now he had to go back in and face the kid named Bycroff and try to get the facts and see who came up with the idea first, who dreamed it up and made it true.

Evgeny Popov

All Heaven Aglitter

Translated by Joanne Turnbull

'What would you have me do with a person who commits all manner of abominations, and then weeps?' (Anton Pavlovich Chekhov)

M me R. O. Scent pressed a lace handkerchief to the moist left corner of her right eye while at the same time reproaching me for having deserted her exactly thirty-three years before when we both resided in the city of K., situated on the great Siberian river Y., which flows into the Arctic Ocean.

'Why I didn't make you out for a rotter right off the bat,' she kept saying. 'Only a rotter could have sent me such an insolent parting letter without a return address. And then write *in that love letter: I enclose a stamp for your answer.*'

'Oh, come now, just your girlish hormones. You wanted to screw and so did I, and why not? By the way, you were a fine one yourself; why did you let that live rooster loose in my room?'

I objected peaceably, patiently waiting for this new Russian lady's fleeting feeling of dejection to pass, for her to be her positive, relaxed and energetic self again. The thing is that we had already drunk some rather pricey vodka, Russkii

Standart, from Rosalie Ossipovna's bar. She mixed her vodka with orange juice, adding exactly two ice cubes to her crystal goblet, as she, evidently, had been taught in America. I just knocked back half a glass neat and chased it with a pickled cucumber. Rosalie Ossipovna Scent had certainly mastered the art in the intervening years of pickling cucumbers, whereas before she hadn't known how to do anything like that, except how to screw and swim in underground caves for money. Rosalie Ossipovna was then a loyal Komsomol member, an athlete and a swimmer. She was called, then as now, Rosa, but she had a completely different last name – what, I simply couldn't remember. It was either Kukushkina or Khristanyuk. I have a terrible memory these days: hardening of the arteries, stiff joints, gout, high blood pressure, gastritis, prostatitis, curtains.

'A dusty road, and bushes beyond, / Wait a bit, you too shall rest anon,' I sang for no reason.

'What?' Rosalie Ossipovna looked surprised.

'It's an idea of the poet Mikhail Lermontov's, which he, in his turn, borrowed from either Goethe or Heine. Heinrich Heine. The Russian poet Lermontov was a Scot by birth, while the German Heine was a Jew. Pushkin was an Ethiopian, Turgenev a Tatar, Leskov an Englishman, Dostoevsky a Pole, and Chekhov, naturally, a Czech. Workers of the world unite,' I explained.

'But who are you? That's what I want to know,' she scrutinized me.

'Me? A simple, Russian, intellectual guy, capable of big things. To be more specific, I could run the culture section of a new glossy magazine. Without politics, with a moderate number of ads and erotica verging on pornography. For a salary of $2,500 a month.'

'You haven't seen this?' she made an obscene but elegant and somewhat provocative gesture. I have to say that she had changed very little over the years. That's what comes of being athletic from an early age, and maintaining a healthy lifestyle; eating right, for example. She was still slender, shapely and catlike. In short, feline.

Her father, Osip Pinkhasovich Scent, had been born in Vitebsk to the poor family of a confectioner. Illiterate, he had figured everything out on his own. Squeezing the serf out of himself drop by drop, he had become a revolutionary, had known Marc Chagall, and served in the Cheka, where he rose steadily up the ladder and would unfailingly have been buried in Moscow's Novodevichy Cemetery next to Khrushchev, say, or Kaganovich, had he not been shot by his own colleagues in 1950 at the height of the campaign against cosmopolitanism.

Her mother, Nadezhda, whose last name was either Kukushkina, or Khristanyuk, was also from a common background, also a revolutionary. But she had been brought to the revolution by love.

The thing is that she had worked as a maid in the house of a depraved Moscow merchant-decadent who was on friendly terms with Maxim Gorky, sometimes gave the revolution a little money when in his cups, and was a sponsor of Stanislavsky's, yet lived in an enormous palace, on the Moscow street Malaya Dmitrovka, in an exceedingly slovenly manner – both morally and physically. A terrible womaniser, he nevertheless took pride in the fact that Chekhov had stayed in this very house before his famous journey to Sakhalin to extol the hard lot of the Russian working and criminal people. He made passes at the housemaid as well, spied on her in the bath, and could not understand why she wouldn't put out, though for that simple act of coitus he had offered her quite a nice sum. A bourgeois gone wild with money and drink, he never realised that in this world there is not only carnal desire but genuine love. He would have roared with contemptuous laughter had he learned that his *housemaid Nadya had fallen in love with an exterminator of cockroaches and bedbugs,* quantities of which were to be found in his filthy house, which is why the terminator was summoned on a regular basis, which is why that love flourished. Time passed, a *player piano* was forever playing in the merchant's house, it was noisy and merry, but devoid of genuine happiness, and he ended by hanging himself in the city of Nice (or the Bolsheviks hanged him, it's not clear which), having left behind a bizarre note, a quote from an early poem tossed off by his friend Maxim, 'Farewell, I said as I raised the sail and took the wheel with a silent wail.' But he was still alive when the housemaid Nadya, while resting one day after sex, was suddenly filled with proletarian intolerance, which is why she suggested to her little cockroachman Osip: 'Let's poison the prick for good with some arsenic, the fat hog, they're making him a meat aspic today and I can slip in as much as it'll take to do the job.'

The underground revolutionary and future Chekist, Osip Scent, shook his head sternly: 'No, Nadya, the revolution must be made with clean hands. I think that snake'll soon kick the bucket on his own. And if he doesn't kick the bucket straightaway, then he'll be doomed to destruction, like any exploiting class.'

And that's just what happened.

* * *

'But you've come through the world's upheavals and anxieties unscathed, just think of it. Communism collapsed, the USSR was disbanded, terrorists blow us up daily with the complete sympathy of fucking besotted left-wing intellectuals. And you're only more beautiful. Before, to be honest, you were quite homely; you wore glasses. Have you started wearing contacts?' I asked.

'Yes,' she said tersely, thinking about something else.

During the post-perestroika years Rosalie Ossipovna had contrived to live in Israel, Italy, England, France and America, but she hadn't liked any of those places, and now she had returned to her fervently loved Motherland, the widow of a celebrated Russian-French avant-garde artist, whom she had delivered in due course from the USSR to the West, but not before taking back her immemorial surname and proving to the thickheaded Bolsheviks that she, the former Kukushkina (or Khristanyuk), now the Zionist Scent, had the right to emigrate to her historical homeland. She participated in demonstrations and pickets, and bravely sang right to the authorities' faces, 'Day and night I will repeat, let my people go!' Under the Soviets, the artist, naturally, had not been recognised; twice he'd been clapped in a psychiatric hospital, though malicious gossips claimed there were grounds. He was seriously eccentric. On their first wedding night he had their bed made up with the party's *dirty tablecloths instead of sheets*, and not long before his death, in their magnificent villa in the ancient French town of Bière-les-Alpes, *he frightened his wife every day after dinner by saying that he would go into a monastery, his wife cried and cried* afraid, to boot, that the loony would leave all his money to that monastery. Sometimes Rosalie

Ossipovna thought that he was probably a latent homosexual, which made her cry even harder. Everything in this world ends. Now his paintings are worth millions, and she is home again. Hello there, Motherland! Hello, sweet capital of Moscow!

'Why didn't you marry me then anyway?' Rosalie Ossipovna asked pointedly and spitefully.

'Just try to imagine. After all you seem to have your feet planted firmly on the ground these days. *There would have been such a poetic wedding, and then – what fools, what children!*' I was trying to be witty.

'What do you mean, what children?' Rosalia Osipovna replied.

'I was speaking figuratively, I mean you and me.'

'*And who're the fools?*'

'You and me again.'

Rosalie Ossipovna grinned and slowly lit a Vogue Menthol.

'No, no. There's a Russian saying about people like you: "He's a real fool, but he wouldn't eat soap".'

'I recently heard another version of that dictum,' I said. '"He's blind as a bat, but he wouldn't eat soap".'

'That's just what I'm saying: you're a rotter. You knew perfectly well I'd been raised in an orphanage for children of "enemies of the people" where everyone teased me. *Even that tiny little schoolboy by the name of Trachtenbauer.* A well-read scoundrel and the son of a Japanese spy, he predicted that I would never marry. I often had diarrhoea and when I did he would grimace and quote from somewhere, *they nicknamed the young lady "castor oil" and it stuck, which is why she never married.* And even so you treated me so meanly, disappearing like that. What cruel people Russians are, that includes you! The Chechens are right to blow you up.'

'Oh, you bitch!' I cried. 'They're right to blow us up, are they? What about in Israel, and in Spain, and the World Trade Center, and "Nord-Ost", and the schoolchildren taken hostage in North Ossetia? So you think Trachtenbauer was Russian? I suppose Ossetian children are Russian too? My ancestors on my father's side, for example, were Kets. Have you ever heard of that nationality? The Kets were Yeniseian Ostyaks, the most indigenous people that ever existed in Siberia, there were more of us than American Indians, to whom we're related, and now there are only 1,202 Kets left, including me. And, yes, I was a fool, but I'm wiser now and I consider that in Russia either everyone is Russian, or no one is, and all sensible people must live in peace if they want to live at all, and not die at the drop of a hat in the name of their ideals.'

'Don't be angry, dear,' she grazed my burning ear with a stiff finger. 'I'm not Vanessa Redgrave yet, Akhmed Zakaev is no protégé of mine. I admit it, I was wrong, and God will punish me for that. Forgive me, but what a woman won't say when incensed. And I've always been and remain a woman.'

'No argument there,' I muttered. 'But you know my neighbour, the alcoholic-cobbler Lazar Pafnutich, would always wail when incensed at his wife for taking away his pay: "*When I married, I became an old woman*"! Well, I haven't become an old woman. What do you think, why is that?'

'Why don't you tell me yourself if you're so sure about that,' she smiled.

'About what?'

'That you haven't become an old woman. After all, that hysterical fit of yours just now was very like an old woman.

Don't argue, I've become quite a good psychologist over the years.'

'With your money you could become quite good at anything,' I retorted. 'I didn't become an old woman because I didn't marry you. And, by the way, I'm still not married.'

'The only reason you're not married is because your last wife finally kicked you out because she couldn't bear to put up with you anymore. Don't think I don't know. I did, of course, make some inquiries about you as my future hypothetical employee.'

'Well, well, you all certainly learned fast from the capitalists how to humiliate working people,' I said.

'What do you mean "you all"?'

'You new Russians.'

'But I'm Jewish,' she laughed.

'You can be both,' I remarked gloomily, because our conversation had reached a complete impasse and my prospects did not look good.

The late child of 'illegally repressed' old Bolsheviks. An orphan. A Komsomol member. A self-made woman, who supported herself by diving with an aqualung in underground Siberian lakes in karstic caves. A dissident. An émigrée. A moneybags. What good and civilised times we had had screwing back then when we both lived in the city of K., situated on the great Siberian river Y., which flows into the Arctic Ocean. She lived in a student dorm at the teaching college, I lived in a warm apartment with a huge library, inherited from prosperous Soviet parents, ordinary people, who lived their whole lives in fear of everything and only shook their gray heads on hearing my seditious adolescent speeches. 'Better keep your mouth shut, or they'll take you away, and we'll have nowhere to run.' Parents whom I lost, just as I did the apartment, just as I did my motherland. Because the USSR was my motherland! I was born in the USSR. Now none of the things listed above exists anymore, there's only old age and Rosalie Ossipovna Scent. Oh, how we loved to *do it* on my balcony in the early morning, when the entire Soviet people was on its way to build communism!

'But still, why did you let that live rooster loose in my room, taking advantage of the fact that my key was always under the mat?' I asked.

'My roommates and I thought you'd appreciate our joke. We swiped a rooster at the market and we thought it would be very funny when you came home to find a live rooster there.'

'It wasn't live for long,' I said.

'What do you mean?' She looked at me wide-eyed.

'I mean I slaughtered it, boiled it and ate it.'

'What for?'

'Not what for, why. Because my nerves were shot. Because,' I sang the words, '*the whole day music played, and our affair dragged on.* Because I couldn't stand communists and yet I'd tried to become a Soviet writer. Because I hated the idiotic phrase that we would see all heaven aglitter. And if I hadn't eaten that rooster, then you would have scarfed me right down, like your artist. Scarfed me down, sucked me dry and spat me out.'

'You really are a fool. A fool and a rotter.'

Again she pressed the lace handkerchief to her moist eye, the left one this time. And I pressed her to me. She exuded a barely detectable scent. We both sank into a sweet somnolence. Rosalie Ossipovna Scent, a publishing industry shark, who had launched a new glossy magazine in Moscow without politics, with a moderate number of ads and erotica verging on pornography! Rosalie Ossipovna, you are so nice. I love you. I have loved you, Rosa Kukushkina (or Khristanyuk), my whole life, fuckit!'

She seemed to read my involuntary thoughts.

'I've always loved you too,' she stammered, her eyes closed.

But then quietly added: 'However, I still won't hire you to work on my magazine. Don't be angry, it's just that there would be too many problems with you.'

Again she made an elegant but obscene gesture. I was dumbstruck. Night had fallen over Moscow, only the Kremlin stars burned bright. Everywhere wild capitalism was in the ascendant, but I didn't care anymore.

'We shall still see all heaven aglitter,' said I.

Courttia Newland

Smile, Mannequin, Smile

The skin was almost perfect, and yet cold. A sunset glow of rusting tan spread across a lithe body. Hints of red dotted in amongst brown. A scattering of freckles running from right shoulder to elbow. A blemish-free face, even in tone. Adams tended the skin using oils rubbed deep into the surface, making it shine with an appearance of good health. There were very few defects, something that never ceased to amaze her. That she, such an imperfect creature, could create something so close to perfection, so unreal.

The morning Mr Yoshimoto came, Adams was almost finished and feeling pretty pleased with herself to boot. Despite the near-perfect result, this one had been difficult; she hadn't made the armature quite right, and her casts of the feet had gone wrong too. She'd had to remold the latter, though when she looked at the mannequin now she knew that only an expert would see the inaccuracies. Her daydreams had consumed her while she worked, and she'd downed a bottle of red wine too, which had probably led to her mistakes. The wine coalesced with her memories; pretty soon there she was, with Frank on her mind once again, *reminiscing about the time she broke a molar on barbecued ribs. She was drunk. They were all drunk.* It had been her wedding day.

The first she knew of Mr Yoshimoto was the realisation that some miscellaneous customer was ringing her workshop buzzer. She left her mannequin and watched him lurk uncomfortably on the bottom right corner of the black and white view screen. He was short and nondescript, wearing a suit, tie and matching hat, some dark colour she guessed. He looked East Asian, though she wasn't sure. He spoke her name slowly and seriously into the tiny microphone, asking if it was possible to spare five minutes. He'd made no appointment. Adams buzzed the man in and waited.

Yoshimoto entered the workshop seconds later, looking up, down and around at the forest of body parts, mouth wide open; then he saw her. He immediately bowed with a deep tilt of the head. Unconsciously, Adams did the same. When they looked up, she could see that his face was large for such a small man, almost perfectly round. She was pointlessly intrigued by her observation.

'Good afternoon,' he said.

'*Domo origato.*'

The man beamed, displaying a jumble of misplaced teeth and pink gums. 'You speak Japanese?'

She smiled in return. 'No, just visited Tokyo for a month. Picked up the basics, that's all.'

'But you try. That is very good.'

Her head was still nodding like one of those puppies in the rear window of a car. She forced herself to stop.

'Thank you. Now, what can I do for you Mr . . .'

'Yoshimoto. Konishi Yoshimoto.'

Adams shot him a look tinged with slight disbelief; tempered slightly, in case she appeared rude. 'What, you mean like the writer? Banana Yoshimoto?'

'Yes, yes; you know her too?'

Adams guided Yoshimoto towards her office space, a small cubicle with a computer and phone in a corner of the work-shop. She drew up a chair and eased him into it while he beamed continuously. She wondered if the knowledge that she'd been to Japan made him so cheerful, or whether he was naturally that way.

'I do, Mr Yoshimoto. So, you begin by telling me how can I help and I'll make the tea. Is that a deal?'

'I accept.'

She flipped a switch on the kettle and retrieved some battered mugs and teabags from a cupboard. When she'd made the tea and turned back to face Yoshimoto with her steaming mugs in hand, he was holding a magazine open on his lap. The pages were all full colour, glossy and brightly presented. Adams used the pretence of putting a mug down beside him to peek at the magazine, but she couldn't quite see what it contained. Yoshimoto was concentrating on the pictures before him with an almost religious reverence.

'I want you to make an Asian doll for me. Like the ones in this magazine.'

She frowned. 'You did check out my website before you came here, right? You know I only take mass orders from retailers?'

'Yes, I read that. But my need will be equally matched by my money, Miss Adams . . . I am prepared to pay £5,000 for your services . . .'

She tried to retain her casual demeanor, but surprise lit up her whole face, Adams could feel it. Before she knew it her arm was outstretched, fingers beckoning.

'Can I see that a minute?'

'Of course.'

She took the booklet from him and opened it. For a long time after that, she was too stunned even for speech – thus, the only sound in the workshop was the rustle of glossy paper as she turned pages. What she'd thought was a magazine was in fact a brochure, seemingly produced to promote the sale of life-sized Japanese dolls. They were fully clothed and placed in a number of 'real-life' poses – sitting by a window, lying on a bed, one even perched on the toilet – still fully clothed of course. It was difficult for Adams not to feel admiration right alongside vague disquiet. Even in a summer dress, a blouse and jeans, the dolls still seemed overtly sexual in their intent; they were cast with breasts, pretty young faces and even what one line of advertising referred to as a 'marriage-hole'. Yet it was the artistry of the unknown mannequin maker's work that really stirred her interest. The faces were so pretty, so lifelike. Adams wondered just how hard it would be to recreate that type of subtle, understated beauty. All the mannequins she'd ever designed had been so obviously false she'd never even considered making them pretty. And of course, there was the issue of earning £5,000 for something that would cost peanuts to make.

She raised her head from the brochure. Yoshimoto was watching her with a focus that was a little disturbing, a little unlike his former cheerful persona. She noted that he hadn't said a single word or drunk from his teacup since he'd passed her the brochure.

'Can I keep this?' She waved the limp booklet.

'Of course.'

'And I'll need half the payment up front.'

Yoshimoto immediately began digging into his inside

jacket pocket. He produced a chequebook, a gold pen and a small, slim-line silver case. He opened the case and gave Adams the embossed business card within with a flourish that only accentuated his pride.

'Call this number when you have finished. It will take how long?'

'I'd give it six weeks or so. If it's gonna take any longer I'll let you know.'

'Finish within six and you get an extra thousand bonus.'

Interesting. She studied the card he'd given her; the title, Konishiwa Enterprises, told her nothing about the business her new client was involved in, but that was OK. She figured the less she knew about a man who wanted to buy a life-sized doll complete with 'marriage-hole' for twice the rate advertised in his glossy little brochure, the easier her job would be. The phone number was local, she recognised that. By the time Adams read the card and placed it in her little desk draw, Yoshimoto had filled out a company cheque for £2,500. He held it by one corner, beaming again.

'You will do a good job, Ms Adams. I have made a great deal of enquiries about this matter. Everyone tells me you are the best. You are even named after a famous doll, isn't that correct?'

Adams blushed, busying herself taking the cheque and putting it in her small desk safe, avoiding his eyes.

'Yes; my full name's Barbara, but I use Barbie for business' sake really . . . It's been my nickname ever since I got into mannequins . . .'

He was watching her with calm focus in his eyes again. She passed him her own business card just to give her hands something to do.

'I have embarrassed you. I will leave now and let you continue your work.'

Yoshimoto got to his feet. She saw him to the workshop door, her mind racing with questions she dared not ask.

'Thank you, Mr Yoshimoto. I'll call in a week, let you know how it's going, OK?'

'I would appreciate that very much.'

He bowed so low she could see his fading crown. Adams did the same, smiling slightly.

'Good afternoon, Miss Adams.'

'*****' She was laughing quietly in disbelief before the workshop door had even closed behind him.

At first, Adams considered using herself as a model for the body armature; she was slim and around five-seven, which she guessed matched the models in the brochure, and she'd save a few hundred pounds too. One long look in the mirror immediately changed her mind. There was no hiding her African figure, even if it came via the Caribbean island of Antigua. She would have to take the search outside her workshop. In great TV-gameshow tradition she phoned a friend, who advised that Adams try the School of Oriental and African Studies down in Russell Square. Within four days she'd posted an ad on the college noticeboard and received six pictures from likely candidates; within two, she was sure who she wanted. Sayaka was a talkative, giggly student from Kyoto. She was taking African Politics, which Adams found highly curious, and had lived in Kenya, Zambia and Ghana over a four-year period before she even came to England. She was the perfect model in all ways; cool and detached, able to sit still and not fidget . . . And of course, she was beautiful too; her skin glowed a creamy butter colour and her pouted lips were like a tiny pink flower, the upper petal slightly larger than the lower. Adams took Polaroids, noting the black beauty spot just above Sayaka's upper lip. She faxed the photo to Yoshimoto for his approval, which was rapidly attained. The women agreed on a price, £300 for the whole sitting, and decided to begin work the very next morning.

Over the next four days, Sayaka attended the workshop every afternoon for three hours at a time, stripping down to her knickers and letting Adams wrap her in bandages like an ancient Egyptian, then pour fine casting plaster over her limbs, torso and eventually her whole head. She was patient and compliant as Adams had judged, blasé about shedding her clothes, which made the whole process that much easier. Adams turned up the heating and kept her eyes on the work. Sayaka's body was shapely in a way she'd never seen before; thin arms, a generous torso, firm yet small breasts. A miniscule waist leading to widened hips, the faintest raindrop curve of a bottom. She giggled a little when Adams applied the plaster down there, but other than that, Sayaka never made a sound. She held herself perfectly still, chest rising and falling imperceptibly, serene features raised to the lights. Adams wondered if the Asian girl could hear her attempts to regulate her own breathing, or whether it sounded as loud as it felt.

Soon, her model was completely cast. After the last session Adams took Sayaka into her little office cubicle and paid her the £300 in cash. It was an awkward moment, both women aware that their reason for meeting had dissipated like sugar in the tea Adams made every day, until they finally reached this point, both aware that they had grown to become friends, albeit temporarily. They swapped numbers and agreed to stay in contact even though neither intended to. This was the London way. Sayaka waved a dainty little hand and left the workshop, her pretty blue and yellow summer dress dancing as she walked. Adams never saw her again.

She waited for the plaster to set, flicked through the brochure, took a look on the Internet for the company website. The daylight in the workshop dimmed until there was none. Silhouettes of severed limbs made dark shadows on bare walls, yet Adams remained at her computer, the open brochure beside her. It would be a tough job, one that she hoped she could do justice to. Yes, the dolls were slightly strange to look at, and their usage was a sobering thought, but she couldn't help noticing how close they were to the real thing. Her time in Japan had been limited – four weeks teaching art to primary-school children in Tokyo. Though she'd partied and got stoned and hung out with a few Japanese, she'd never seen any women as up-close and personal as Sayaka. She'd always thought East Asian women beautiful, especially the Japanese, yet the true extent of their splendor had never penetrated her psyche. Now, looking through all the pictures of varied dolls, she realised how flaw-less the real thing could actually be.

In order to finish by Yoshimoto's deadline, Adams decided to work nights and sleep amongst the disembodied limbs, heads and torsos, which wasn't unusual for her. Fuelling herself with more tea, she used copper pipes, mechanics hose clamps and a bench-mounted vice to create a skeletal torso based on Sayaka's dimensions; a laborious and sweaty task. Still, she'd always found the bending and tugging therapeutic; a chance to think and maybe even realign her Chakras, if such a thing were possible. She turned on the radio for company's sake rather than a desire for music, and once again found the voice of the presenter drowned out by her own inner voice, her own memories, which never escaped her head; they simply buried themselves deep in the flesh of her brain, waiting for moments like these to scratch their way to the surface, bawling for attention. And so she was assailed by recollected thoughts that came in tandem, one leapfrogging to another, from her hen night, to her broken molar, to her wedding night (a stoned disaster) and subsequent honeymoon (Butlin's). To be perfectly truthful, the only time Adams ever thought about Frank, her estranged husband, was when she was hard at work. She guessed that was when the barriers keeping him out of her conscious brain fell back like flood gates, letting the waters of her recollections rush through and tear down everything representing her present state of mind. He had been a weak, unruly man, addicted to drugs more than her, whereas she'd used them as a temporary escape, nothing more. They were together three years before the penny finally dropped; he wasn't going to change, even if she did. She was twenty-four years old with a chance to start again. The day she finally left the squat Adams had been plagued by the thought that she'd never see him again. Now she knew what she'd taken as a staunch realisation had in fact been hope.

She lived on the hard wooden floors of vague friends and acquaintances for months after that, and was accepted into Saint Martin's Art College the following year. She was given her own room and a shared bathroom and kitchen within halls, the first space she'd ever had a chance to call her own. Though the building was filled with students of all ages and nationalities, Adams kept pretty much to herself, reading, cooking and attending the odd Art Exhibition if her studies and funds permitted. There were a number of Japanese students who formed a tight group like the fingers of one hand creating a fist. Adams' curiosity was raised by their cheery manner, their quiet politeness and easy beauty. She began to hang out with them, though never to any great degree. When she graduated she kept in contact with one, a quietly crazy yet talented twenty-one year old named Junko. That was how she learned of the teaching job in Minowa. On her return home, Adams knew that she'd rather practise art than teach it. She applied for the first job that came her way, an apprenticeship at a mannequin workshop in West London.

Adams' life was shunted onto a new, not entirely un-familiar track. Her mentor, Barry Megson, was a cold, clinical man who rarely had time for smiles or even jokes; which suited her just fine. He taught her everything she knew today, there was no doubt about that, but apart from the lessons in plasterwork they rarely spoke. She fell deeply in love, first with Megson, then with the art of mannequin making. They slept together once and decided never to do it again, Megson claiming he loved his wife and didn't want to complicate matters. Adams, wanting to hold on to her job more than her fleeting love affair, let him go without a fight. When Megson died a year later from a sudden asthma attack, Adams was both shocked and grateful to find that he'd left the workshop to her in his will. His widow tried to contest, but there was nothing she could do – everything had been legally certified. Adams ignored her phone calls and threat-ening letters until they trickled to a slow halt, and threw herself into her work; so much so, the only friendships she formed were work related. Her only pleasures likewise.

Once the armature was finished, Adams wrapped it in chicken wire and carried the skeleton into a small back room behind the main workshop, sitting it up against a large plastic bin filled with soaking clay. She spent two hours spreading an even layer of gloopy substance all over the chicken wire until it was completely covered. This would anchor the weight of the sculpture to its copper skeleton. Next step was to cast the doll using Sayaka's body mould. This took three bags of Herculite number two plaster, with some left over for the feet, hands, arms and legs. The hands and feet were made using Alginate casts of another model, a lanky Australian teenager she'd met in the tea section of a Turkish supermarket in Harlesden. The girl, Alex, had the most surreal, elongated fingers and toes Adams had ever seen, which looked almost Alien in real life, but became beautiful and elegant when cast in Herculite. She didn't normally use the same model for hands as well as feet, but since she'd found Alex there'd been no need to look elsewhere. All that left was the wait for Sayaka's body parts to dry, which took another day, and the attachment of metal fittings for the wrists, waist, shoulders, and neck. This would allow Adams to add movable limbs and a head.

By the beginning of the fifth week, when she'd completed sanding and added the final touch of skin colour, Adams was forced to smile at her handiwork. The doll looked undeniably sexy. Placed beside her previous mannequin, the difference between the two was amazing. From a distance, Sayaka looked good enough to mistake for a real live human being; she could even be – and here Adams balked at the thought – as lifelike as a work by the late Duane Hanson. It was the attention to detail, the little imperfections all human beings possessed, that made her new creation so perfect. Forcing down her pride, not even allowing the thought to grow roots, she tentatively spread some extra plaster on the mannequin's rear to make it more pert, reading a book while Sayaka dried. It seemed fitting that she'd chosen Murakami; she'd ordered *Sputnik Sweetheart* over the Internet years ago but had never got round to reading the novel until now. The concise, simple poetry of his prose brought back pleasant memories of Minowa; the tale, concerning Sumire's infatuation with Miu, drew her in easily, like dipping a toe in warm bathwater. She dug out some traditional Japanese CDs bought during her month in the country, and drank green tea from the local corner shop. When the torso was dry she went back to work, getting out her brushes and paints and mixing a deep yellow colour that almost bordered on brown. Of course, the paints had to be modified to fit the original colour of the mannequin, but she achieved the effect she wanted within an hour. Adams painted well into the night before falling asleep on an old sofa she'd dragged into the workshop. The next day, she continued her task.

When everything was finished, including facial make-up set off with pale-pink lipstick and black eyeliner, Adams opened a box that contained yet another Internet purchase – a shiny, almost blue-black, shoulder-length wig. She had searched long and hard for East Asian hair, and was referred to a small company near Carshalton by her regular Wandsworth supplier. Slowly, breathing lightly, Adams walked over to the mannequin, which had taken centre stage on the workshop floor, away from the other mannequins. As gently as she could, she placed the wig on the bald head and at once burst into an involuntary giggle, one hand lightly touching her lips. She stepped back, a broad smile flooding her face.

'Hello, Sayaka,' Adams breathed, unaware that her mouth had even moved, let alone that she had spoken. Yet she had voiced the truth. The doll was now the spitting image of the Japanese student. The closest to a human being Adams had ever created.

She rang Yoshimoto the next morning after spending another night sleeping in the workshop. He didn't seem at all put out at the prospect of shelling out an extra thousand pounds, sounding as cheerful and lively as she'd expected. He told her he would arrive at her workshop by early after-noon, 1 p.m. at the latest. Adams nodded and put down the phone without an answer, feeling a little tired around the eyes, a mite pensive. She'd been unable to stop herself waking during the previous night, standing before her mannequin, unable to stop herself from shaking her head in pride, though not without a little incredulity. It was truly difficult to believe that Sayaka had come from her own hand. The doll was her best work ever, real enough to have been born of the womb. She'd run her fingers up and down the cold arm, along the line between her breasts, even fingered the hard depth of her marriage hole; putting this last intru-sion down to morbid curiosity. She regretted the hole as soon as she'd finished drilling and couldn't imagine why anyone would want to violate beauty in such a manner. Nevertheless, it was done now, and done to Yoshimoto's specifications. How she felt about such things was irrelevant.

He rang the workshop bell at five to one. It was raining by that time and he came inside with tiny droplets sprinkled on his head and shoulders like dandruff. He seemed agitated or somewhat hurried today, bowing quickly and shedding his black Inspector Clueso raincoat before she could even complete her Japanese greeting. His actions caused her to frown; she couldn't stop herself, which Yoshimoto couldn't help but notice. He explained that he was suffering from a full bladder and requested the use of Adams' lavatory. She ushered him halfway there, both of them pointedly ignoring the object that stood in the centre of the workshop floor, draped in a sky-blue dustsheet from head to plastered toe. Walking back into the workshop, Adams heard the lock click and the toilet seat clatter. She looked at the concealed mannequin once more as she crossed the room towards Yoshimoto's raincoat. She had very little time.

She knew that what she was about to do was crazy. The thought only occurred when Yoshimoto walked through the door; the only thing that remained had been the how, until he took off his raincoat and rushed into her toilet. Such divine providence only came along once in a while. Adams reached into his jacket pocket and there they were; Yoshimoto's keys complete with a blue BMW tag. Moving fast, her ears straining for sounds of the businessman's progress, she grabbed the first piece of clay she could find, flattened it with one hand, and then pushed each key into the soft lump, one by one. Three almost perfect impressions were left, lined one beside the other like fossils; a house key, some other miscellaneous Yale, and his car key. Quickly, she trotted to her battered sink and washed the keys off before putting them into his raincoat, being careful to make sure she returned the bunch to the exact pocket she'd found them in. She hid the lump of clay in a desk draw and then sat on the first available chair, crossed her legs and picked up a trade magazine. Yoshimoto came back five minutes later looking pale.

'Are you OK?' she asked, being as polite as she could, honestly worried by the pallor of his face.

'Something I ate disagreed with me,' the businessman admitted, looking forlorn. 'These bloody business brunches will be the death of me.'

'Would you like a glass of water? I have Alka Seltzer too.'

'Yes, yes, you're very kind. That would be marvellous.'

'I'll just show you your mannequin, then I'll fix it right away,' she told him, walking over to the dustsheet and unveiling Sayaka without waiting for concurrence. She was watching him the whole time; yet even if she hadn't, Adams would still have heard his sharp intake of breath when he laid eyes on her creation; the long exhalation that followed, like the slow release after orgasm, impossible to stem or control. Ignoring the involuntary shudder that ran through her, she smiled brightly and said, 'I'll get your water,' but he wasn't hearing her, Adams could tell by the way he stared blindly at the counterfeit Sayaka as if nothing else in the room was there, nothing else in life mattered, and it was then and only then she was secure in the knowledge she could not do this, could not let perfection go. After all, it was her creation, made with her own hands. Sayaka belonged to her.

She made the Alka Seltzer and brought it to Yoshimoto, who drank it down in one go just like he should. Still holding the glass, still staring up at Sayaka, he seemed unable to grasp words. He stepped forwards, touched her face and hair. Adams looked at the floor.

'Is she what you wanted?' she asked, when her heartbeat slowed to an acceptable pace.

'More,' Yoshimoto replied, and she could feel his sincerity. 'Have you named her?'

'Sayaka.'

'Perfect,' he breathed. The word was hardly audible.

'Yes,' Adams said, still looking at the dusty floor. 'That's what I thought.'

They replaced the dustsheet and carried Sayaka to the BMW, Yoshimoto taking the head and Adams the feet. He opened the boot, placed the doll inside, shut it with a satisfied smile. Adams tried to match it, but couldn't muster enough feeling, even when he gave her a cheque for the remaining £3,500. Her gaze kept inching towards the boot of the car like metal ball bearings attracted to a magnet in their midst.

'You are a genius,' Yoshimoto told her. 'I have many friends who would enjoy your work. Can they call you?'

'Of course,' she said, of course – though the weight of each word bowed her head as though there was a giant hand at the back of her neck, pushing hard. Yoshimoto stood before her, stiff and formal.

'It has been an honour to meet you.'

'An honour to meet you too, sir.'

He was gone before she knew it, the BMW easing out of the industrial estate, leaving her with an ache she hadn't felt since she was a teenage girl.

* * *

She had a local locksmith for a friend, someone who'd long fancied her from afar. Therefore, the keys were cut within the hour. All she had to do then was head for the address on Yoshimoto's business card, another industrial estate just off Scrubbs Lane. She took the train to White City, avidly reading *Sputnik Sweetheart*, and walked the rest of the way, the newly cut keys sharpened splinters in her pocket, all rough edges and hard lines. She was fully aware that what she was doing was a) highly irrational, b) highly illegal, and c) highly stupid, but she couldn't stop herself. Somewhere in the back of her mind she even knew that she should wait, think this thing out before going off on such a sudden whim; but she could not. Only very rarely did Adams get an urge as strong as this. It wasn't even so much an urge as some primal instinct long buried, which emerged just like her memories. Whenever it came to her Adams always found the instinct impossible to dissuade. Like when she'd left Frank. One day she'd woken up to a morning no different from any of the others and known it was time to go. Didn't need to pack any bags because she had nothing to take. Simply got out of bed, left him sleeping on his stomach dead to the world, opened the front door and walked, never to return. Because she wanted to. Even today, those four words added together equalled the clearest reason she could remember.

It took at least twenty minutes to get to the right place, another fifteen to find the road and a further five to climb to the top of a steep hill, where the industrial estate was situated. This one was a lot newer than the place her own business inhabited, Adams reflected; where hers was made up of old buildings with cracked paint everywhere, steaming pipes and narrow overhead walkways, this one had long detached units that looked like overgrown garden sheds, separate car bays outside each one, huge shuttered doors. Taking only the smallest glances left and right, Adams headed for unit 51, the address on Yoshimoto's business card.

She found the car easily, parked in the relevant bay. The surrounding units were silent, and apart from the odd fork-lift truck, no other vehicles went by. The hairs on the back of her neck stood to attention. Every step was filled with hesitation as she approached the BMW, the car key hidden in her hand, waiting to hear the alarm at any moment. When it went off, Adams' minuscule plan was to grab the doll, run back down the hill as fast as her legs could carry her and hope that someone judged the alarm false. She had long dismissed any thoughts of CCTV or of being caught in the act of stealing. The only thought that crossed her mind was of Sayaka.

She ran her fingers across the smooth, black bonnet. No alarm. She pushed the key into the lock, turned it slowly as she dared, heard the click as metal rubbed against metal. No alarm. She lifted the boot lid above her head, aware of every slow creak. When it was fully open and nothing happened, she was assailed by another, more recent memory; Mr Yoshimoto knocking back the cloudy fizz of Alka Seltzer and looking at her, grateful as a dog receiving a bone. He'd been sick hadn't he? Maybe even sick enough to hurry back to work without setting his car alarm?

Adams was just reaching for the blue dustsheet when a man behind her spoke.

'What d'you think you're doin'?'

She turned slowly. The security guard was wearing the generic beige shirt with matching creased trousers and brown shoes shined to a mirror finish. He had a walkie-talkie and a cloth badge that told everyone his occupation but, thankfully, no gun. He was burly, black, and not bad looking either. Adams kept her face down, embarrassed by the strength of the accusation before him.

'Mr Yoshimoto . . .'

'Mr who?'

The guard was still frowning; even so, she wanted to run over and hug him tight, plant a big smacker right on his juicy lips. The two words he'd spoken might as well have been life and line.

'Konishi Yoshimoto. My boyfriend. He wanted me to get something out of his car for him . . .' She waited a moment, looked into his eyes, and raised her freshly cut keys.

'. . . Even gave me his spares . . .'

The burly guard stared, then made a rapid decision.

'Come inside a minute, let's sort this . . .'

'But . . .'

'Let's go . . .'

She put a hand on the boot lid, heart wrenching in fear in the sudden acceptance that she was heading for more trouble than she'd ever been involved in – when a crackle of static roared abruptly from behind her. Her heart leapt once more. When she turned back to face him, he was glaring into the receiver of his walkie-talkie, one hand on his hip like a cowboy.

'*Zero-one, Zero-one.*'

More static, before a voice emerged from deep within the crackles like a woodsman fighting back the thick of forest.

'*Zero-one, this is Zero-five; could you immediately report to the Grey room?*'

He looked at her balefully when he replied, but she could tell she was saved in an instant; the anger in his eyes was a clear indication.

'On way Zero-five; over and out.'

'*Over and out.*'

He put the walkie-talkie back on his waist belt.

'I'll be checkin' up on you,' he snarled.

He left Adams holding the boot lid high above her head, whispering a prayer beneath shallow sips of halted breath.

Hefting Sayaka beneath one arm, Adams got on the first bus that arrived, which would take her as far as East Acton Underground station. From there she would catch the Central Line back to her workshop. Once upstairs on the old Routemaster, Adams removed the dustsheet from the doll, positioned her limbs so that she could adequately sit upright, and turned her head to the left so that Sayaka could look out of the window. She looked much better for it too. Yes, people were staring, but after all it was a free country, wasn't it? They were just as entitled to stare as she was to ride on the bus with a mannequin friend. She wasn't going to be ashamed, and if people thought that was strange behaviour, well that was up to them. She even found courage enough to put one arm around Sayaka as the conductor warily approached. Adams looked up into his craggy face, beamed the cheeriest smile she could muster and asked for two to East Acton please.

Andrew Crumey

A Lesson for Carl

Ten years old, walking with his father to the street in
Vienna where they were to find his new piano teacher: the
best in the city. No one else would do for young Carl, such
a prodigy, with his miraculous young fingers curling in the
pockets of his coat as the two of them, man and boy, made
their way down the cobbled lane. They walked quietly; Carl
was too nervous for conversation. So too, perhaps, was his
father Wenzel; since both of them had heard so much about
the man they were to visit.

Their silence was interrupted by the clatter of horses'
hooves behind them; Carl's father gently pushed him away
from the edge of the road as a wagon passed, spattering mud
from a puddle at them as it took its cargo of old furniture
along the narrow residential street and then around a bend,
out of sight.

'Be sure to play your best today, Carl,' his father said.

'I will,' Carl promised. Already, at that moment, his whole
life was mapped out ahead of him, though he didn't know it.
Fifty-six years later, on his deathbed, people would still want
to know only one thing. What was he really like, this man
they were about to visit?

There, on a corner, stood old Krumpholz, smiling when
he saw his two friends approach.

'Are we late?' Wenzel Czerny asked anxiously. He was a man who loved good discipline in life as much as in music. He considered punctuality a matter of honour, and lack of it a disgrace.

'Never fear,' Krumpholz reassured him. 'I got here early. But now we should go and see Ludwig.' He glanced down at Carl. 'Did you bring your scores?'

A look of terror flashed across Carl's face; the unbounded fear of a child who thinks he might have forgotten something vital, finding himself at the mercy of his elders.

'He doesn't need them,' Carl's father interjected. 'He will play from memory.'

'Very good,' said Krumpholz, pointing the way and then starting to walk with his two companions. 'Ludwig always prefers his pupils to play from memory. He learns a piece in no more time than it takes him to play through it at sight. Though I have to admit,' he lowered his voice and his face, addressing Carl with a twinkle in his eye, 'Beethoven is somewhat apt to make mistakes.'

'He plays false notes?' Carl's father said incredulously. 'Even before an audience?'

'Certainly,' said Krumpholz, softly taking hold of Carl's arm, and then of his hand when the lad freed it from the pocket where it had tightened with the same dread that afflicted his stomach. With his leathery thumb, Krumpholz coaxed the boy's fingers until they unfolded and surrendered to his comforting, grandfatherly grasp.

'You see, Carl,' Krumpholz added, 'even a virtuoso can play in error, and all is forgiven. I heard Ludwig play one of his own concertos, and there were many passages that lacked the polish a good student would apply. No, to hear the real musician in Beethoven, you need to listen to him improvise. Then, my boy, you will be taken to another world – one you will never forget, as long as you live.'

As he lay dying, old and venerated, Carl would recall the accuracy of this prophecy.

'Now, here we are,' said Krumpholz. 'This is the street where he lodges.'

It was called *der tiefe Graben* (the Deep Ditch). It was a name that would stick in Carl's mind, with its suggestions of dirt, of the grave. Things you can spend a lifetime trying to avoid, perhaps through the liberating qualities of music. Yet in all the concerts that lay ahead of him, in the great career on which, at ten years old, he was already embarking, Carl would never escape the deep ditch where it all began.

Krumpholz was leading them across the road, then through the open doorway of a tall apartment building. 'I hope you don't mind if we take our time,' he said, indicating the stairwell. 'Beethoven unfortunately lodges on the sixth floor. Not a problem for you, young Carl, if he takes you as his student. But I do wish he'd find lodgings in a place where an old man like me could visit him more easily!'

Slowly they began to ascend. It was Krumpholz who had first told Carl's father about Beethoven, Vienna's new musical genius. Krumpholz played violin in one of the city's theatres; he knew all the local figures, and had made Beethoven's acquaintance almost as soon as the young virtuoso arrived from Bonn. That was a decade ago – around the time when Carl Czerny was born. And his father Wenzel, seeing the swaddled baby helplessly burbling, had resolved that he too, this child blessed with the infinite potential of life's beginning, would make his own equal mark in the world.

What had happened in those ten years? In Beethoven's case, some concerts and publications, and the making of a name. Anyone who knew about musical life in Vienna was familiar with Beethoven's work. To admirers like Krumpholz, he was a miracle; the true successor to Mozart and Haydn. To others, his chamber compositions were merely a random outpouring of fragmentary themes, lacking in discipline. He was said to be working on his first symphony now: perhaps that would make more sense.

And what about Carl? The last ten years had made not his name, but something infinitely greater: his soul, his entire being. The previous decade, the 1790s, had been his whole lifetime, and Carl's father had watched the boy's development with the patient satisfaction of a gardener seeing the spreading limbs of a tree. Already Carl could play Beethoven's sonatas from memory. What else might he be capable of, in another ten years?

Above all, Herr Czerny knew the importance of starting early. Beethoven was twelve when he gave his first concert. It was, Krumpholz once suggested, perhaps a little late: hence those mistakes Beethoven was apt to make in concert. And contrary to what Krumpholz claimed, Herr Czerny knew there are always those among the impassive faces of an audience who do not forgive; there are those who remember, take note, and arm themselves with the latent ammunition that will eventually topple a career. Ten years from now, where would Beethoven be? Forgotten, perhaps, and replaced by a new generation of surer hands, more dexterous fingers, quicker minds. Young Carl, his father felt sure, would be at the vanguard of that generation.

Having slowly ascended the gloomy staircase, they had

now reached Beethoven's door, its green paint cracked and peeling. Krumpholz knocked, and a moment later a man opened it. Was this the master? Carl's immediate impression was of someone too scruffy, too humble in appearance. But no, this was not Beethoven. 'Come in,' the shabby servant said curtly, allowing them inside.

They were shown into a room which was like an inanimate version of the servant; equally untidy and neglected, and just as inhospitable. There were several men standing waiting, but Carl dared not stare at them, and instead found his gaze traversing the papered walls, stained in places with damp, lacking any picture or mirror. The striped, faded wallpaper was torn and in need of replacing.

Then there were the trunks and boxes carelessly arranged beside the far wall, as if the lodger had only just arrived, or expected to leave soon in a hurry. And the piles of paper – Carl saw printed music and manuscript pages, many of them strewn where only the soles of visitors' feet could have anything to do with them. If he ran out of sheets of paper, it seemed Beethoven would resort to any other surface. Even a dirty tablecloth, Carl noticed, bore a scribbled memorandum.

He saw broken quills, spilled inkwells; and as Carl took in more and more of the scene, its squalor only deepened. Was he to come here as a pupil?

Would his father leave him undefended in this place on whose floor the occupant had thought fit to toss a soiled shirt and a discarded coat?

Despite the clutter, there were few real furnishings in the room – the shortage of chairs explained why everyone was standing, though after ascending so many stairs they all could probably have done with a rest. One item alone lent a redeeming air of civilisation to the proceedings. In the very centre of the room there was a piano, the instrument on which Carl would shortly be tested. He stared at its open keyboard, a sight as unsettling to him right now as a tooth-puller's pliers.

'The best there is,' Krumpholz whispered to him, momentarily breaking away from the round of adult greetings and introductions, which their arrival had prompted. 'A Walther – lovely piano. I do hope he's had it tuned. Ludwig isn't always kind to his instruments, you know.'

Carl was too young to fathom the delicate financial equation that had placed such an item of luxury in a setting of virtual poverty. A less magnificent piano would have equalled more chairs, a polished table, and other costly surfaces in which the assembled company, if they had wished, could have seen reflected the bourgeois tastes that gave them all a living.

But they were here for only one reason: the same reason that the piano was here. They were musicians, scraping a living in a world that valued them only as a soothing background to genteel conversation. Here at least, in Beethoven's lodgings, their art was treated with respect.

Krumpholz was tactfully offering Carl's father, whom he had drawn aside, a hushed synopsis of all the social information with which Wenzel Czerny had so swiftly been bombarded over several handshakes.

'That's Ludwig's brother,' Krumpholz explained in a whisper loud enough for Carl to hear. 'He takes care of Ludwig's business arrangements – and does so very competently, I believe. You see, genius is all very well – but there has to be a commercial brain as well. And that man – yes, the portly one – no, not him; I mean the one who's really fat. That's Schuppanzigh, the violinist. He and Ludwig admire one another artistically; but to be perfectly honest, I don't think they really get on. And that one there, Sussmayr, he was Mozart's pupil. Yes, that's right – it was he who completed the *Requiem*. So you see what an audience has been assembled for your son!'

Overheard by Carl, whom all the men ignored, these words were hardly reassuring. Like any child, he had to remain silent until the moment came when they would want to listen to him.

Then at last, something happened. 'Here he is,' someone said. And Carl saw a new figure enter the room; someone straight out of the book he had been reading that morning. It was Robinson Crusoe.

The newcomer was stocky, strong looking, with the snub nose of a fighter. His complexion was darkened by the sun, his chin was unshaved, and the thick black stubble made him look like a savage. He had come from the dangerous wilderness of Carl's imagination, and now he was standing close in front of the lad, towering over him, placing a hand on his shoulder by way of greeting.

'Say hello to Herr Beethoven,' Carl's father instructed. Carl tried to form a greeting, but found his throat dry. The nervous crackle that emerged drew laughter from the adults.

'Ssh!' Beethoven raised a finger, silencing them. The back of his hand was hairy; his whole body must have a pelt like a bear's, Carl imagined. The locks on Beethoven's head, black as coal, were thick and uncombed.

Strangest of all, though, was the detail Carl would still

recall vividly many years later. There was something sticking out of Beethoven's ears.

Wads of cotton, steeped in yellowish fluid. Was it perhaps a joke designed to make Carl laugh? Or was it a way of avoiding sounds the composer didn't wish to hear? Whatever the reason, nobody else appeared to notice these silly cotton ears. Nobody knew, in fact, that the thirty-year-old composer had recently begun to experience problems with his hearing.

Carl saw kindness on the face of this swarthy Crusoe, as if the lonely man recognised in his young visitor a new companion, a pet, who would share his island domain. But Beethoven's face grew harder, more determined, as his gaze rose from son to father. 'Let's not waste time,' he said in an accent which, to Carl, sounded foreign and mildly ridiculous. 'Show us what the boy can do.'

Beethoven went and stood with the others while Carl sat himself at the keyboard. Then Carl launched into the piece he had prepared: a Mozart concerto. As he began playing, his nervousness left him; everyone else in the room quickly disappeared. The stained walls, the soiled clothing, the discarded pages – all were magically washed away by the waves of music that came from beneath Carl's fingers. The instrument was perfect; the finest he had ever touched. It stood on a tropical beach, and behind him was Robinson Crusoe, picking the remains of a freshly caught fish from his teeth.

The wild man softly drew up a chair beside Carl as the boy embarked on a series of delicate arpeggios. There was no orchestra in this island paradise; instead, Carl's companion began to touch the keyboard with his own shaggy hand, his fingers blunt as chisels, yet infinitely delicate.

Beethoven was filling out the harmonies of the concerto with his left hand, while Carl continued the solo part.

All the burdens of his father's ambitions were lifted from Carl's shoulders as he moved effortlessly through the concerto, swimming aloft while Beethoven continued to accompany him, tugging gently with notes and chords that kept Carl anchored to a steady beat. When it ended, there was silence. Carl felt his bodily weight return; and with it, he experienced the swift restoration of all his anxieties.

Beethoven stood up and addressed himself to Carl's father. 'He plays well, but I want to hear him in a solo piece. Make him give us a sonata.'

Carl looked up at his father, who nodded in confirmation of their prearranged plan. Then a moment later, Carl struck the opening chords of a work that had only just been published. It was Beethoven's own *Pathétique* sonata. Carl felt a murmur of surprise and approval from the onlookers, then silence again as they let him perform the first movement from beginning to end. This time there was no desert island, no Robinson Crusoe. Instead, Carl was on stage before hundreds of people, a grown man, showing everyone exactly how the piece should be played.

All great art is a vision of the future; and Carl was being granted such a vision now; an ineffable foretaste of his destiny. Ten years from now, Beethoven would be the most famous composer in the world, and Carl Czerny his most famous pupil. Another twenty years, and Beethoven would be dead, while Carl would be revered. The decades rush on – until Carl himself lies dying, sixty-six years old, his mind clearing for a moment as he looks from his bed towards the light of the window, a grey drizzle, the memory of his first visit to the master who gave his life its greatest meaning. When the boy finished playing, Beethoven spoke once more in that rustic accent of his, brought from his native Bonn. Addressing Carl's father, he said, 'I shall take him as my pupil.'

Carl had passed the test. He saw his father beaming broadly, and he felt profoundly relieved. His mother, too, would be smiling when they told her, equally grateful to have been spared the calamity of failure.

'Well done,' Krumpholz was saying, shaking Carl's father by the hand. The other men joined in: all congratulated Herr Czerny on the triumph of having produced such a son.

Beethoven interrupted, concerned only with practicalities. 'Be sure that when he comes to me next week he has C.P.E. Bach's book on keyboard playing. We'll start with the positioning of the hand.' Carl's father promised that they would buy the book at once. 'And another thing,' Beethoven added. 'Don't make him practise too much. Let him be a child. He'll grow up soon enough.' He looked at Carl, speaking properly to him for the first time. 'You're lucky to have such a kind father,' Beethoven told him.

'Yes, sir,' said Carl, wondering what sort of childhood Beethoven must have had.

'Now we must leave,' his father instructed. 'Come along, Carl, we need to go to Sterner's bookshop.'

Carl saw that the music making in Beethoven's lodgings was set to continue. Schuppanzigh had started tuning a violin, and Beethoven was seating himself at the piano. Carl longed to stay and listen, but his father drew him by the hand, outside onto the cold stairwell, where the servant closed the door on them without a word.

'What did you think of Herr Beethoven?' Carl's father

asked him as they began to descend the stairs.

'He's too hairy, he's got a funny voice, and I don't know why he has to stick things in his ears.'

Wenzel Czerny laughed. 'I agree he's an eccentric character. But they say he's the best teacher in Vienna. You did well, Carl. One day perhaps we'll look back on this moment, and see it as the most important in shaping your career. Doesn't the future look bright?'

Above them, the music was beginning. Carl could clearly hear the violin; the piano was softer, with only a few booming notes drifting down the stairwell. While Carl had played, the future had indeed seemed bright. Now, hearing fading music from behind a closed door, he was less sure. His life, he suspected, would be an endless, arduous climb; and at every moment he would fear falling to his doom.

They came out onto the street, where fine rain had begun to fall from the grey sky above. A coal wagon was trundling past, and the grown-up world was going about its business. His father was eager to get to the bookshop to put in an order for Bach's manual – Carl's homework for the next year or so. And suddenly, from above the clouds, it was not rain Carl felt dropping onto his face, but notes of music. They were Beethoven's: little black notes melting on his face, moistening his coat, gradually puddling on the ground, slowly drenching the street.

That's what he saw at the window now. Not the fine drizzle he had thought, but those notes of music that fell on him as a boy. He felt the urge to say something; but as with his greeting to Beethoven more than half a century earlier, old Carl Czerny found his throat to be dry and voiceless. He couldn't call the maid, or his wife. Nor could he move the arms and fingers that had been taught by the master and had premiered his works. At the age of sixty-six, Carl Czerny was about to die alone.

Yes, he was revered: but only as a teacher and performer, not as a composer, as Beethoven ultimately was. Carl had never lived up to his father's aspirations, had never outgrown his famous master, but had instead been supplanted by his own pupils – people like Franz Liszt. Too disciplined, they called him; too polite, too shy. His destiny was already fully scored when Robinson Crusoe patted the ten year old on his head. The notes were tumbling out of an infinite sky; they were dripping through the ceiling, onto the bed where Carl lay dying, and he opened his mouth to taste the black notes falling on his tongue. It was what he had spent his whole life trying to avoid: falling into the deep, dark ditch. Stumbling, playing a note that was false. Yet there they were, millions of them, carelessly cascading over the entire world. Krump-holz had been right, all those years ago. Clumsy Beethoven was forgiven. It was Carl Czerny who was damned for his accuracy, his modest fidelity. Rising into the sky, he thought for a moment of how he might have done it all differently. But Beethoven's first lesson to him was also his most accurate. Don't practise too much. Let the child be a child.

Julia Darling

The Dress

Rachel stood in the shadowed hallway, screaming her sister's name over and over again.

Her thin body was taut and tight, her whole body shook. 'Flora, Flora!'

No one answered. The silence held its breath. She wiped her eyes, though she wasn't crying. She wanted to spit.

Rachel stamped up the stairs, pushing open the door of her sister's room, wading through disordered heaps of crumpled discarded clothes, empty cigarette packets, broken lighters, dried-out mascara brushes and lidless lipsticks. It smelled sweet and slightly rotten. Rachel wrenched the half-closed curtain back, so that the room was suddenly filled with floating specks of glistening dust. She snatched handfuls of clothes from half-open drawers, throwing them onto the floor. She knew that she wouldn't find the dress. Flora was wearing it, sitting outside a café, blonde hair falling across her eyes as she laughed, flicking ash onto the ground.

Rachel walked back into the blue kitchen, with its neat bowl of shining apples on the long table, and the purring silver fridge. She stared at the place where she had left the dress, ironed and ready to wear that night for their mother's birthday. The hanger was still there, thin and wretched, but the dress had gone, and the room smelled of Flora. There were other signs too. A cupboard door was still open. There was a warm smell of cooked noodles, an unwashed bowl in the sink.

Rachel picked up the hanger and threw it onto the floor. She wanted to hurt someone.

At one end of the table was a neatly folded pile of used wrapping paper left over from that morning, when Flora and Rachel had sat watching their mother opening her gifts. Cards were displayed on the mantelpiece, most of them with either cats or flowers on the front. The mother was at work now, and for a moment Rachel imagined her sitting opposite a distraught client in a cream-coloured room, pushing a box of pink tissues across a coffee table. Their mother was a bereavement counsellor.

That night they were going to an expensive restaurant. It was their mother's fortieth birthday, and Rachel knew that she would have to be pleasant, to forget about her stolen dress, wear something else, and smile. The thought was unbearable.

She sat in the fading afternoon, wired up, white faced. She tapped her red nails on the hard table and closed her eyes.

Flora was wearing the dress. It felt delicious, like water. The dress was made of thin silk, weightless and elegant. It was light green, with golden ribbons around the hem and the neck. As Flora walked through the hot city she felt airy and delighted. She had wanted the dress ever since Rachel had pulled it from a carrier bag and pranced about with it held to her sharp body. It had made Flora's mouth water, just looking at it. It seemed to Flora that the dress was meant for her, not Rachel. It made her feel taller, braver, cleverer, and Rachel was all those things already.

Usually Rachel locked her room and guarded her things carefully, so when Flora had found the dress hanging in the kitchen, available, her eyes had widened with pleasure. She had reached out and stroked it, glancing over her shoulder to make sure there was no one else there. She lifted the soft material to her face, inhaling its scent of confidence. At first she had simply thought that she would try it on for a moment and then replace it, but once it clung to her young body she found she was unable to take it off. She walked around the empty house, rejoicing in the way the dress made her feel slim and long legged.

Then Alberto had called round, and told her how beautiful she looked in the new dress, and before she knew it she was slipping out of the house, a bag hanging over her shoulder, arm in arm with her Italian friend, feeling sophisticated and elite. She would return the dress later, she thought. Rachel would get over it. And that night it was their mother's birthday and Rachel wouldn't be able to shout at her.

The restaurant was modern with long white tables and huge blown-up photographs of petals and stamens on the white walls. Waiters stalked between the busy tables, holding bowls of mussels high about their heads and pouring wine wrapped in white napkins into high-stemmed glasses. Rachel and her mother arrived together in a taxi, and Flora arrived later, flushed and apologetic. The mother saw how Rachel hardly looked at her sister. She sat stiffly in her chair studying the menu, wearing a harsh black dress and bright red earrings. Flora was crumpled and colourful in a blue silk shirt and white cotton trousers.

The mother sat between them, nibbling olives, talking incessantly, aware of the hollow silence between them. She read the entire menu aloud in a surprised voice. Flora listened, head on one side, while Rachel scowled.

The waiter brought a basket of bread rolls, a bottle of sparkling wine, and took their order carelessly.

'What's the matter?' asked the mother eventually, buttering the edge of a white roll.

'Nothing,' said Rachel.

'Cheer up then,' giggled Flora, scattering crumbs across the white tablecloth. 'It's a celebration.'

The chatter in the restaurant was almost deafening. In the centre of the room there was a colourful, boisterous party, who kept exploding into wild shouts and shrill laughter. The mother was aware of a woman who was squeaking, 'Larry, don't do that. Please!' She wanted to turn and see what it was that Larry was doing, but felt glued to her two silent daughters.

The waiter brought prawns fried in garlic, soup and asparagus, and fiddled with their forks and spoons.

'This is lovely, isn't it!' exclaimed the mother.

'Can I try some asparagus, Rachel?' asked Flora.

'No,' answered Rachel.

The mother's head ached. She wanted the meal to be over. She wanted her daughters to make an effort. She filled up her daughters' wine glasses and raised a glass in the air.

'Larry, leave off!' squawked the woman.

'I wish she would shut up!' snapped Rachel.

'What are you angry about?' asked Flora in a lightly whipped voice, as she chewed a prawn.

'You know why I'm angry.'

'Why?' asked the mother, spooning her soup around her bowl.

'The dress,' said Rachel, unable to contain herself. 'I want the dress back.'

'I don't know what she's talking about,' said Flora.

Behind them a glass smashed on the floor.

'Yes, you do!'

'Did you take Rachel's dress, Flora?' asked the mother in a thin voice. She suddenly wished they had gone to the cinema and sat together in silent darkness. Communication between her daughters was often like this; barbed and dangerous. She coughed.

The waiter whisked away their plates, leaving them with nothing to do.

'Did you?' asked the mother again.

Flora laughed and wiped her mouth. She looked around the restaurant as if expecting to see someone she knew. Rachel shook her head slowly.

'Can we stop talking about it?' asked Flora. 'It's mother's birthday.'

'I'm forty,' said the mother. She felt sorry for herself. All day she had sat with tearful needy people. It was her birthday, and she wanted to relax. She wanted to feel loved.

The waiter appeared with three large white plates, on which small portions of meat and fish were arranged.

'I just want to know where it is,' said Rachel suddenly.

'I never took your fucking dress!' shouted Flora. The noise in the restaurant subsided.

'Flora!' whispered the mother, who wanted life to be calm, a flat sea with no sudden breezes. She liked emotions to be explored in safe rooms, with a clock.

* * *

149

Rachel cut into her steak. It oozed red blood. I am leaving, she thought. I never want to see my sister again. This thought sustained her and she lifted her glass, saying 'Happy Birthday!' and smiling for the first time that evening.

'I'm so old,' said the mother.

'You're not!' said Flora.

'No, not old,' said Rachel.

'I think I might leave my job,' said the mother.

'I thought you enjoyed it,' said Rachel.

'It's just so sad,' said the mother.

'What would you do instead?'

'I thought I might make something, like jewellery.'

The two girls stared at their mother. She had some strands of soft grey in her black hair and faint lines around her eyes.

'Jewels,' repeated Flora, dreamily.

The loud people on the table behind them started to sing HAPPY BIRTHDAY, DEAR LARRY! It made the mother feel belittled. She pushed her plate of tuna fish away.

'I don't want pudding,' she said, rather childishly.

Later the three women returned to the tall house behind the park. The mother opened a bottle of wine and lay on the sofa, letting her shoes fall to the floor. Flora sat curled up in an armchair and told her mother about a film she had seen. They could hear Rachel moving about upstairs.

'What's she doing?' asked the mother, and Flora shrugged.

Rachel had packed a suitcase. She called her father and asked if she could stay with him. He sounded surprised, but told her that he would leave a key under the rosemary bush as he was going to bed early. When she replaced the phone she could hear her mother and sister laughing in the sitting room.

Rachel put the suitcase in the hall.

'Rachel, come and have some wine,' called the mother.

She put her head round the door.

'What are you doing?' asked Flora, innocently.

'I'm going to Dad's.'

'Why?'

'Because I can't live here any more.'

Flora jumped to her feet, spilling a drop of red wine on the carpet.

'It's that dress isn't it?'

'Where is it?' Rachel leaned against the doorframe.

'I don't know.'

'But you do.'

'Please, Rachel,' begged the mother.

'You ask her.' Rachel sat down.

'Did you take the dress, Flora?'

Flora sat on the floor. Her eyes were slightly tearful. She shrugged.

'See!' exclaimed Rachel.

'Did you?' asked the mother, sitting up, concerned.

'It's only a dress,' whispered Flora, 'only a scrap of material.'

'But did you steal it?' The mother sounded like a teacher, harsh and unforgiving.

Flora began to sob. She hid her face in her hands, her shoulders shaking. The mother pushed a box of tissues towards her.

'Why did you do it, Flora?' asked Rachel.

'Because I loved the dress. It was so pretty.'

'Where is it now?'

'You'll hate me.'

'I hate you anyway,' said Rachel.

'I was with Alberto, in the Café Malata. We were drinking cocktails.'

The glass had slipped out of Flora's hand. The drink was bright red, with glassy slivers of ice and fruit. The front of the dress was stained horribly. She and Alberto had dabbed and rubbed the stain with napkins, but it just made things worse. Flora had felt cold and frightened. Then Alberto had to leave and Flora was all alone, the dress sticking to her skin, the sun gone.

She had come home, tiptoeing into the house, afraid of meeting Rachel, but she wasn't there. Flora had peeled the dress off, held it under the tap, but she knew it would never be clean again.

'So what did you do with it?' Rachel sounded defeated, almost uninterested.

'I buried it in the garden.'

'What?' exclaimed the mother.

Flora had taken the wet dress outside, and found a trowel. An icy wind blew the leaves from the trees. Weeping, she had dug a hole at the bottom of the garden, among the magnolia bushes. The earth had smelled of dead birds and empty houses. She had buried the dress, covering it with soil, then kicked dead leaves over the disturbed ground.

'You see,' said Rachel to her mother. 'Nothing is safe. That's why I'm going.'

The mother shook her head again and again. Flora was twisted into a knot now, afraid to look up. A taxi hooted outside and Rachel stood up.

'Happy Birthday,' she said, and walked out.

As soon as the front door slammed, Flora sat up and looked at her mother.

'Don't be angry,' she said, in a childlike voice.

'I am very angry,' answered the mother. 'Everything is ruined. You are a thief.'

'I know it was stupid.' Flora leaned her damp head against her mother's leg, but the mother stiffened and pulled away. She stood up, walked to the wide glossy window, and pressed her face against the glass, watching the taxi slide away.

'Please,' said Flora to her mother's back.

'I want you to dig it up and give it back.'

'But it will be all dirty,' moaned Flora.

The mother was suddenly furious. She turned on Flora with flashing eyes.

'You will pay your sister back!' she snarled.

But Flora looked genuinely perplexed. It was only a dress, she thought, hardly a matter of life and death.

The mother grabbed Flora and shook her shoulders. Flora pushed her away.

'Leave me alone!' protested Flora.

'I want you to leave!' sobbed the mother.

'Don't worry. I'm going,' said Flora. She pulled on her jacket and ran out of the room.

So the mother drank the rest of the wine and sat looking out at the black night, listening to footsteps in the street of people coming home from the bars in lively skittish groups.

And the dress lay in the tired earth, smelling of dead birds in a porch in an empty house, and was forgotten.

Rajeev Balasubramanyam

India Isn't There

11.30 p.m. Thursday, 22 July

I cleared my desk and left. On the street I found a skip and tossed everything inside. I felt four pounds lighter.

Every day I lose another layer. People keep telling me I've lost weight, but soon I'll be transparent, able to soar into the air like cellophane. No one will notice when I do.

I have earned the right to fly, although, in thirty-four years I've achieved nothing. One ex-wife, several ex-girlfriends and no children; a handful of stories in magazines, now recycled, and then these serials that no one remembers. I don't think it's even possible to watch them in a conscious state. I told this to William when I resigned.

'That's the beauty of it, Somu,' he said. 'You're making a mistake, my friend. You're becoming precious.'

He's wrong. I'm the opposite. When a man knows his worth to be zero he can fly.

I finished my errands. Closed my account and converted my savings into traveller's cheques. Stopped by my estate agent. Everything's fine. My furniture is in storage, my house empty except for a mattress and hot-water bottle. A sold sign lies in pieces in my front garden, broken by the gale. British weather is an evil thing. I'm becoming rheumatic, in bones and mind.

Then, last of all, the one I had been looking forward to. Only one airline would do. I remember at cricket matches, India versus England at Lords, whenever a plane flew overhead the crowd would rise as one and yell, '*Air India!*' (even when you could see the letters 'BA' as clear as if painted on the seat in front of you).

I remember one game when I wore a paper hat with the words, 'Tebbit go home. I am an Indian and fucking proud.' There I was, chanting for India with thousands of others, and I'd never even been there – not that I remembered, at least.

When Nasser was captain, ten thousand people would chant his name. 'Nasser is an Indian,' they'd shout. 'It's a fucking disgrace,' I heard someone say. 'Born in Madras and playing for England.'

I was also born in Madras. My twin brother never made it, and the doctors said I was gone, but then my cold little body began to breathe. Plucked from the jaws of death, I was a happy, healthy child. My mother said I only began to cry when I came to this country, and then I stopped, for twelve whole months when I needed it most. But that's another story.

Now my family are dead. My brother, of course, my sister, and my parents too. I have the address of an uncle I've never met and, with no children to my name, this is all that remains of me, and it's there, in India. I tried to tell the idiot at the embassy this, but he gave me a three-month visa. He said, 'Do you know what we go through when we come to your country?'

It makes no difference. On landing I'm going to burn my passport. At thirty-four I want to fly. I want to never cry again. Who knows, perhaps three months will be enough. A butterfly lives for hours, days at best, the bulk of its life spent preparing for those moments of beauty.

1 p.m. Friday, 30 July

Drinking coffee at the airport lounge, I cannot keep my mind on my journal. Airports seem to attract the prettiest girls (only the beautiful can fly?) but this is something deeper.

I like to think I can tell from the face. Countries leave their imprint and this girl, I have decided, is from India; born and raised there, that is, with matching accent and sensibilities. This attracts me. With the exception of my wife, all the girls I've dated have been Asian, but never from India itself – or herself, I should say.

She's sitting with four companions, all male. From their body language I conclude they're no more than friends. Perhaps they study together, returning home with a degree from the University of British Life. Let me check.

I was wrong. She is British, very much so, her accent educated and without a trace of otherness. Watching her now I'm still entranced, but by the familiar in place of the exotic. Her four companions seem less innocent now. But I'm making too much of this nationality thing. That isn't why I'm going to India.

My coffee is cold and they're announcing my flight and she and her bodyguards are rising. I let her go. There's plenty of time left before we reach Delhi, and there's some-thing I have to do before I leave. Let me put down my pen and rest my head on my elbow. They will think I'm dozing, but no, this isn't the time for sleep. You can join me if you like. Before I fly, my last, ever, weep.

3 p.m. Friday, 30 July

The plane took off late. One of the engines had fallen off, I think.

Looking around, I'd say this flight is less than fifty per cent Indian. Backpackers, package tourists, hippies and a large number of people who, I suspect, are going for some form of work. I'm imagining herds of empty suitcases like skinned elephants, ready to return with bellyfuls of relics and knick-knacks for sale in Camden at astrological prices. India is big business, I'm starting to realise.

I can't see the girl. Maybe they aren't on this flight. Indians don't have to go to India. Take me, for example, I've been all over the world, but never to the one place that mattered.

It'd be too easy to blame my wife. She once told me she was so relieved I had no connection to India. When I pressed her she clammed up, but I know what she meant. My mother always wanted a daughter-in-law she could speak Tamil with. I think my wife was terrified of being out of place, of being exposed as, well, as herself. And then there was the question of children –

I just asked for a second whisky and the steward told me, 'But you've already had one whisky.' He's bringing it now, but I can see him muttering under his breath. This isn't the friendliest of airlines. The man on my left asked if there was somewhere he could pray, and they told him, 'Pray in your seat, but don't disturb anyone.' By this, I think they meant, 'Just close your eyes and pretend you're praying.'

The man on my right is reading *The Economist*, and a woman a couple of rows down keeps asking about the sky phone. The sky phone's only for Business Class, she's been told. She doesn't look happy.

That gives me an idea. Back in a minute –

I was right! My lovely lady is in business class. She must be rich. Perhaps she *is* from India and the accent is the product of schools and weekend trips to Oxford Street. India's middle class, I read, is growing, though in some states life-expectancy is as low as two.

I wonder how long I've got. My health is poor, my funds limited, and my passport says three months. But still, if butterflies lived forev

5 p.m. Friday, 30 July

'Can everybody hear me? This is not a hijack. We are not terrorists. We have no political or religious agenda, and we are not thieves. Our weapons and masks are for security purposes only and will be discarded at the appropriate time.

'It may reassure you to know that we have instructed the gentleman to my right to record every word I say. In this way, the truth, our only objective, may be preserved for years to come.

'The truth. You have been led to believe you are on board the AI547 from London, Heathrow, to New Delhi, India. But this isn't true. Ladies and gentleman, this plane isn't bound for Delhi and never was. The truth is that *no* plane is bound for India. And why? Because India isn't there!

'Quiet, please, ladies and gentlemen, quiet please. I repeat that, contrary to all appearances, this is *not* a hijack, and your patience *will* be rewarded.

'The sub-continent we know as South Asia, ladies and gentleman, including Pakistan, Nepal, Bangladesh *and* Sri Lanka, was destroyed approximately seven years ago. It has been a long-held agenda of the ruling elite to eliminate the region by supplying India and Pakistan with warheads of a destructive capacity as yet unknown to all but this elite and a handful of scientists in Washington.

'Though we are uncertain as to the reasons for this action, the strongest possibility is that this act of *genocide* was nothing more than a weapons test along the lines of those conducted at Pokhran though, evidently, on a far larger scale.

'Of course, it has been necessary to maintain the *illusion* of India, and this apparent miracle was achieved by relocating a percentage of the region's population to a simulated India located, we believe, underground, beneath the USA itself.

'This flight, and others like it, was bound for this location. Before landing, we would have encountered an artificially induced storm guaranteeing near-zero visibility, before plunging through the earth's surface in the Nevada desert, and emerging in the new New Delhi airport. You, ladies and gentlemen, would have landed convinced you were in India. The pilot of this flight, AI547 to New New Delhi, can confirm every word and in due course, when he is ready to speak, will do just this. If this is not enough to allay your scepticism, we have now redirected this flight to the location where India used to be. If words are not enough, and I see from your faces they are not, then perhaps your eyes will succeed where your ears have failed.

'Our intention is this: to set this craft down on one of the few islands that now constitute the diminutive archipelago of New India, a land mass no greater than that of Wales. When the authorities arrive we will surrender peacefully and you will be returned to your point of origin. Heathrow airport, London.

'Let me repeat: we are not terrorists and this is not a hijack. Enjoy the rest of your flight.'

1 p.m. Friday, 31 July

When they came, my first thoughts were of the girl. Had they harmed her? What was happening behind that curtain?

Five of them, wearing black ski masks and carrying flick-knives. Of course, 9/11 came to mind. Where would we die? Half way up the Eiffel Tower, or the Tower of London? Maybe the Colosseum. Call me a bigot, but I imagined beards beneath those masks.

I hardly listened at first; it was only when they appointed me as scribe that the truth began to penetrate. They were Hari Krishnas. It was the only explanation. Krishna transported the entire city of Dwaraka across the ocean, didn't he? And Hari Krishnas took these stories literally. I met one in Islington who told me Rama lived for three thousand years and how did I explain that? Well, I don't believe it, I replied, and he'd looked surprised. That was it – I'd been abducted by vegetarians.

But these vegetarians were strong. Remembering 9/11, I decided to try my luck and found myself face down on the carpet with a knife handle in my back. That shut the other passengers up. I've never been much of a fighter. The man next to me, I noticed, went on reading his *Economist* – I could see him while my face was on the carpet.

The flight continued. And it did seem we were heading east. The man to my left sought permission to pray and, this granted, reached into the luggage rack for his prayer mat and compass. Afterwards he sat with the compass in his lap and whispered, 'We're going the right way. We'll be over Slovenia soon.'

I nodded and kept my eye on his compass. East, east, east. Night began to fall and, hypnotised by the needle, I fell into a dream.

When I awoke, the sky was lightening.

'Iran,' my neighbour said.

I looked, expecting a Persian carpet beneath me, but it looked like any other landscape.

'It's Iran,' he continued. 'Trust me. I know about flight paths.'

I looked around the plane. My other neighbour was *still* reading his *Economist*. I wondered if he even knew we'd been hijacked. Many were sleeping. A few talked in low voices, but there was little indication of panic or conspiracy. Our captors paced the walkways, knives out of sight, masks firmly in place, and then, minutes later, proceeded to serve dinner which, in spite of our circumstances, was excellent.

'Not the usual food,' my neighbour said.

'You think it could be poisoned,' I whispered.

'Who cares?' he replied.

I agreed, and ate in silence. When the plates were cleared,

the following announcement came over the loudspeaker:

'Ladies and gentlemen, this is your captain speaking. Officially, I am no longer in charge of this vessel. I have been instructed to tell you the truth and, having no option, will do so. Our original course was for Nevada, USA, but instead we will be landing on an island in the new Indian Ocean that used to be India.

'Please remove your life jackets from under your seat and fasten them securely, placing the whistle around your neck. Fasten your seat belts, ensure your seat back is in an upright position, and assume the emergency position with your head between your knees. We are beginning our descent.'

I looked down. Water all around us. My neighbour put down his *Economist* and began to shout.

'We're going to drown. I'll kill you, I'll sue you. This is the bloody ocean, for Christ's sake. Take us to India. For the love of God –'

'India isn't there!' I snapped, and hit him hard.

For a moment I thought he would pass out, but he simply stared at me, his panic turning to bewilderment. Perhaps he thought I was one of them. Perhaps he was waiting to wake up. I didn't care so long as he was silent. Mass hysteria was the last thing we needed.

The plane began to dive. It felt steeper than usual and my ears throbbed. The man to my left put his head between his knees. Perhaps, this time, he really was praying.

I closed my eyes and thought of India.

2 a.m. Saturday, 1 August

A monkey is watching me from a tree. Except it isn't a tree. It's a minaret, but so overrun by creepers it looks natural.

As we stepped off the plane, I saw three men, all Asian, all armed, and waiting for us, though this time with guns. When they saw our captors they broke into a run before embracing them with evident relief. Looking around me, I realised they had been hard at work.

Behind us, they had cleared the undergrowth and positioned lanterns to form a makeshift runway. It was a gargantuan effort, though our pilot must have been skilful to negotiate the landing; he was accustomed to flying into a hole in the Nevada desert, after all.

Further surprises were in store. Our captors, aided by some of the more energetic passengers, unloaded our luggage and built fires over which they suspended pots. As the fires grew hotter (the day itself was scorching) they removed their ski masks, realising, at this stage, that disguise was no longer necessary.

I should have realised. One of them had breasts, and now a sonnet of black hair. She was one of them. Five non-terrorists and one non-male. I caught her eye and she smiled at me. I watched while she and two men donned diving gear and stepped towards the water's edge. As she sank beneath the sea it felt like watching the sun set.

Behind me, some of the passengers were stretched out beneath the sun, dozing. I saw that same man, still reading his *Economist.* My other neighbour had walked away from the gathering and spread his prayer mat on the beach. It was a moving sight, watching him pray, as though I were looking into the very distant past, a fissure between civilisations, the old in ruins, the new wrapped in mist, perhaps never to arrive.

In time, food was prepared but, having no appetite, I stared at the water's edge, waiting for her to return. When she did, it was an anti-climax. I'd expected something from a Bond film, but instead she half-crawled, pulling off her scuba gear and wrapping her hair in a towel before walking into the trees behind. Her comrades called after her, but she continued. I could hear her crying.

I waited, then slipped away in the direction she had taken.

Though night was falling, I had no difficulty following her. I'd like to say her sobs were melodious, poetic, but they weren't. It sounded horrifying in this wilderness, as if we'd lost everything but pain. I'd come to India to escape this, but there I was, like a moth to a flame.

We reached a low hill and she began to climb. I followed as, still crying, she pressed on to the top. Once there, I scanned the mountainside, but couldn't see her. She must have stopped crying. I saw only the water all around us, a canopy of trees, and, to my surprise, a stone building in front of me, half-obscured by creepers and moss, two deer watching me from beside it. I headed towards it.

Before entering, I took out my lighter and flicked it open. When the flame settled, I cried out in shock. It seemed the floor was carpeted with death, a thousand contorted faces, staring up at me. Was this where they died, I wondered, frozen by the impact? I bent down, trying to find a free space for my feet.

The faces were cut from iron. Hundreds, maybe thousands of them, covering the floor. Against the far wall I saw a small shrine, with flowers and unlit incense inside. Moving closer I saw a plaque with the following words inscribed. *For those who live on without knowing they live, and For the millions who sleep beneath the water. India is there.*

And beside the shrine, sitting on the floor, was the girl, her tear-stained face turned towards me. I sat beside her, saying nothing, and we remained like this for some minutes.

'I'm Lakshmi,' she said, breaking the silence.

'Somu,' I said, as my lighter expired.

'Is this your first time in India, Somu?'

I laughed, before realising it wasn't a joke.

'I've never been here before. Or to the other place, if there is another place.'

'Everything we told you was true. That should be obvious by now.'

I nodded in the darkness.

'Why did you want to come here?'

'I wanted a new life, I suppose.'

'But you're Indian, originally.'

'Yes, I have an uncle here.'

'No you don't. Your uncle is dead, or else he's in Nevada, which is as good as dead. There are forty million of them there. The living dead, we call them. And another million who know the truth and say nothing, like extras in a film.'

'A million, and they keep it secret?'

'Do you think anyone would believe them?'

I hesitated.

'You have to see it with your own eyes. That's the point.'

'What did *you* see?' I said. 'Under the water.'

'What do you want to hear?'

She was right. I wanted to hear, 'The Taj Mahal,' shimmering like the drowned Ophelia.

'The truth,' I said.

'I'd need a cigarette for that. Do you have one?'

I gave her a cigarette and coaxed a last breath from my lighter.

'You're not allowed lighters on flights anymore,' said Lakshmi.

'Security must have been sloppy.'

'There was no security, not for this flight. They were our people.'

'Your people?'

Her hand was almost touching mine. I could feel its warmth.

'What I saw,' said Lakshmi, 'was mainly rubble. A few cars, some buildings, almost intact. And then I saw skeletons. Thousands of them. Their clothes were gone, even their shoes. There were children, babies. I always thought the truth would set you free, but it doesn't. It's just the truth. There's more to it than that.'

'Where are you from?'

'Does it matter?'

'I suppose not.'

'I'm from the ocean,' said Lakshmi. 'So are you now. We're already dead.'

I paused, then said, 'I used to see my dead sister in the water, at least I think I did. But no one really dies, not if you remember them.'

'Maybe.'

'I feel like crying now. I told myself, before I came here, that I'd never cry again . . .'

'Cry if you want to,' said Lakshmi. 'I won't stop you.'

And she laughed, the first time I'd heard her laugh, but

then I couldn't hear her anymore.

It was gunfire, loud as if right beside us.

8 a.m. Monday, 1 November

It was dark when we reached the beach, but the fires were still burning. Around them were bodies, a hundred faces turned towards the moon. The plane was gone, the radio too, and all the passengers were dead. We checked for hours, looking for anyone who still clung to life, but they'd been shot with precision, through the heart or the head.

Lakshmi says they must have come by boat. She wonders if they'd known all along.

I asked her if anyone would rescue us, but she shook her head. Her comrades were dead, those on the outside as good as. The illusion had to remain intact. That was all the authorities cared about.

We weighted the bodies, dragged them out into the ocean, and let them sink. It seemed appropriate. It gives me no shame to say that we searched them thoroughly first, taking everything we might need from cigarettes to boots to much needed matches. I have read the *Economist* four times now, cover to cover – India's software industry is booming, I am told.

My three months have passed and my visa has expired. I have no idea if anyone will ever read this journal, but I will continue to write, from time to time. It's a need for me still, even here.

Who knows, next time I write, I may have news for you. Perhaps a child, and then another and another and civilisation will begin again, out of the ruins, out of the ocean. This seems to be the way of things.

For now, I have no regrets. I am glad I came to India, to *this* India, and I'm glad I'm with this woman. In London I used to ask myself the same question every day. 'I've got how much longer?' But now it doesn't seem to matter. We will go on.

India, I tell myself, is here, living, breathing, beneath our feet.

Andrew O'Hagan

Foreigners

Aunt Jessie made a special effort to mispronounce our names, just to stress her hatred of my mother. She liked to sit for hours in the kitchen smoking those terrible Woodbines, chewing the air between puffs as if appraising the air's goodness to breathe. It was all part of some ceremony of impatience on the part of Aunt Jessie, at the close of which she would open her mouth to free a volume of smoke, followed by whatever unkind words had been brewing in her head all day. 'They have no business naming you all after precious stones, or exotic flowers, or birds from foreign places with giant beaks. I don't mind telling you: it's a piece of nonsense. They must think the rest of us were born in a sack of potatoes. Sean's a good enough name for a person, or Bridget, or else Fergus, like your uncle Fergus. Now, I'm asking you. What in the name of the child Jesus is wrong with being a Fergus?'

'People only laugh at a Fergus.'

'Well, let them laugh until the air stops in their throats,' said Aunt Jessie. 'You will soon be ready for St Michael's and you'll sail through your mathematics and all the exams that prove you're nothing ordinary, laughing at people's nice names. I advise you to keep your brains immaculate. You'll soon be the very boss of your teachers, Amanda.'

'Amaryllis,' I said.

'Exotic bird. Person of colour. Whatever it is.'

My aunt said this and took my hand. 'Your lines on here are more Irish than Scottish,' she said. 'One of them goes on for miles. It is very bad. It shows the journey away from the Holy Cross.'

'That might be quite interesting,' I said.

The kitchen table was made from an old barn door and Aunt Jessie began knocking the wood, soon as I said what I said. The television next door and the buses outside, the world indeed and its famous possibilities, were made silent for a while by the fury of her great knocking. When the noise finally stopped, when Aunt Jessie's hand came to rest on the table, my lips were covered with a soft dusting of flour. A bowl of fresh eggs sat between us. They were Glaswegian eggs: more than usually small and white and not quite oval; they had shoogled in the bowl when the table was thumped. 'You'll keep a civil tongue in your head,' said my aunt. 'Heathen that you are. Person of colour. Whatever it is. I'm still strong enough to give you a good kick on the backside and watch your black eyes tumbling down the stairs.'

I was a child then, and could oppose Aunt Jessie only with an army of private imaginings. The day in question, I thought of the Glasgow eggs cracking open and spilling out of the bowl to advance over the old barn door. It would be one egg after the other travelling to meet her fingertips, then moving upwards to coat the skin of her arms and touch her face. Nothing would stop the flow of her catechism – not the eggs' insides, anyhow, which might choose to advance over Aunt Jessie's entire body in a manner quite unnoticed by Herself in Favour of the Nazarene. I should look south and see the egg running down her American Tan tights onto her carpet slippers. I should then look at her face to see what happens. But nothing happens. She continues to mention eternities to be spent in the bad fires of hell, her sticky fingers drumming the table. I see that her lashes are slicked to the skin around her eyes, and she looks surprised in the cold kitchen light, no doubt beginning to wonder why I chose that day to teach her the vengefulness of eggs. That was a long time ago (I thump tables myself nowadays), but a book I've started reading with my students says that people may never recover from the things they have imagined in their lives. The whole thing came back to me the other day, when I went round to Aunt Jessie's house to help her get rid of my uncle's things.

The whole point of Aunt Jessie lies in her love of being ill. 'You never know when you're going to drop dead,' she often says, and for years she has spoken about liver salts and miracle cures, as though being ill was a larger way of being alive, having knowledge about the dangers and making a little more room for yourself in a world of diminishing returns. Mother said Jessie must have thought she'd hit the jackpot when the doctors called her in to say my uncle Fergus was terminal. 'What unbelievable luck!' said my mother. 'Just you watch her now. She'll never be back from Boots the Chemist. She'll be marching up and down the Main Street with a solemn face, to get the new tablets. "Oh my heart is broken," she'll say to anyone who'll listen.' My mother was a bad person, of course, and rather married to her own aches and pains, but she had a point about her sister's secret pleasure at the prospect of distress. Jessie had always been like that. She loved pain and its daily demands. She loved Boots.

'You're a person and a half,' she said to me when I turned up at the house. 'There used to be young women like you, ten a penny in County Cork,' she said. 'Nice white blouses. Curly hair. They didn't know the dangers either.' Jessie was still formidable with her plaid skirts and smokes. As she spoke these words about the women of her youth, I glanced around the room and noticed, through the arch, that her kitchen table was no longer a barn door but a metallic gurney from Ikea.

'Will we go into Glasgow?' I said. 'There's a new Chinese restaurant they were nice about in the *Evening Times*.' She looked at me like I was setting out to test her. 'Right,' she said, and after forty minutes she came back down the stairs wearing a grey scarf and summer sandals. 'It's too cold for those shoes,' I said.

'My feet get itchy.'

'Well, sprinkle some talcum powder on them and we'll find some good cotton socks.'

'Is that what you lecture at the university?' she asked.

'Common sense.'

'Ha ha,' she said. 'Talcum powder and feet. That's your specialist subject for those gullible Americans.'

'No, actually,' I said. 'It's German philosophy.'

She stabbed the air between us to underscore her victory and then wiped her mouth.

'German philosophy,' I said again.

'I've got a good ointment for that,' she said.

In the restaurant, the leaves of a spider plant tickled her neck and she complained of too much ice in the vodka. She wouldn't have wine and she hated fizzy water. 'Wine's not meant for the Scottish,' she said. 'It gives you acid. You have to go in and ask for Nexium for that if it gets bad. Or else Tagamet Plus. That's the more common one.'

'Just one glass,' I said.

'Never you mind,' she said. 'It's the slippery slope for the Scots. They can't digest wine.'

'But you're Irish,' I said.

'That's right. And I'll never drink wine.'

She sat for a while making faces at a tropical fish tank. You can always tell when Aunt Jessie is preparing herself for something big. 'There's no need whatsoever for anybody to live like that,' she said. 'Under water all the time. With blue stones and yellow stones. It's a nonsense.'

'It's a fish,' I said.

'And who decides what colours they like?'

'It's just a nice thing to look at.'

'Not for the likes of me. It's just a way of making people feel depressed about their own lives.'

'Aunt Jessie, it's a fish tank!'

'Mark my words,' she said. 'It's cruel. Those fish were never meant to be here. They resent it. They don't like the damp weather and they absolutely hate the smell of food.'

While she searched in her bag for a mint, I noticed Jessie's gold rings had disappeared from her fingers. She said she had given them to Our Lady of Good Counsel. 'There's girls in the parish have babies and no husbands,' she said. 'Ten a penny, I'm telling you. Not a man between them.'

'Modern times,' I said.

'I'll give you modern,' said Jessie. 'They don't have the right shampoo. The babies' heads are jumping with lice.'

'Not all of them.'

'Yes, Amanda. All of them. All the babies in the parish

whose mothers don't have men have lice. And there are no
proper bottles to feed them with either. Hardly a single bottle
between all of them babies. And none of those cleaning
machines – sterilisers.'

'They're not expensive.'

'If you've no steriliser for bottles, you know what you get?
You get germs. The children are all sick as parrots.'

'That's bad news,' I said.

'I've never heard worse,' said Aunt Jessie. 'Because you
can get things to kill germs, if only you keep your eyes open.'

'Sterilisers.'

'That's right. And the girls of the parish have none, so
we're selling things up at the church to raise the money.'

'That's a nice task.'

'No thanks to the men, wherever they are.'

I asked her if she missed her rings and she sucked in her
cheeks and held up her hands. 'Gone,' she said. 'You've got
to make an enemy of germs!'

My aunt Jessie is instinctively racist, and I see it must be
part of my own enjoyment of tension and disorder that I
always take her to foreign restaurants. 'Tell that one to turn
off the Calor Gas,' she said. 'The fire. It's too hot and it's
making my ankles swell up.'

'Tell him yourself,' I said.

'No, you tell him. He won't do it for me. They like nasty
young people like you. They're always trying to marry girls
like you, girls with a nice clean passport, just so's they can get
to stay here for good and sponge off the social security.'

'That's rubbish, Jessie. They're more Glaswegian than you
and me. They were born here.'

'Don't you believe it,' she said. 'I wasn't born here but I

wasn't born yesterday either. Those ones want your passport. They'll pretend to love you: next minute – they're off.'

'Rubbish.'

'Aye well, Amanda. You just stick to your university books. Half the wee girls up at the school have kids to these ones. I've seen them with my own eyes and none of them is getting any wiser. You have to watch out.'

'Aunt Jessie!'

'I'm telling you. At least half. All the ones with no sterilisers. All those germs in the milk bottles. It all started off with these Asian ones and their liking for passports. You'd think there was enough babies in China.'

'Anyway. You gave your rings to the church.'

'That's right. Wedding band as well. Your uncle Fergus had a good heart and he would've hated this business with the germy babies, just like I do. You've got to put a stop to ugliness.'

My boyfriend from America was the point of this talk. She would never mention his name, never mention Miami, yet all the time she mocked the Chinese I knew she was really saying how much she hated Ben. 'People meet these men on holidays,' she said. 'They get drunk at those hotel discos and wake up with babies. That's what happens. Then the men come here, and after that they all run away.' Eventually I put my keys down on the table and told her to shush.

'Stop it, Jessie. God hates this kind of talk.'

'Don't bring Him into it.'

'Well, stop,' I said. 'You're only offending the Lord. Do you want to be doing that? Because that's what you're doing.'

'He's not bothered,' she said.

'Don't you believe it,' I said. 'God hears everything. And he loves everybody. That is what the philosophers would say.'

'Don't talk rot. They were all heathens.'

'Just the smart ones. But, anyway, the logic of the thing . . .'

She wouldn't let me finish. She just gave herself the sign of the cross, then looked me in the eye with her wise look, the look that says, 'I'm about to tell you something you've needed to know for a long time.'

'Those people you admire all died of venereal disease,' she said.

Aunt Jessie liked to pretend she disliked all food except the stuff she prepared herself, but it wasn't true, she loved restaurant food, and was known to chomp her way through the hors d'oeuvres with the kind of precision that can only come from experience. Eating prawn toast and several spring rolls, she began to reminisce about Uncle Fergus, saying how different he was to other men. How decent he was. How clean. 'What happened to his passport?' I said. But Aunt Jessie didn't mind that sort of remark, familiar enough with her own bad character to find other people's quite convivial.

'It's under the carriage clock,' she said. Then all was quiet in the restaurant, fish swimming, waiters smiling, before a tiny crunch sounded inside Jessie's mouth. It was half way between a crunch and a crack, perhaps more of a snap. Her eyes instantly filled with tears as she began to pull out a long barbecued rib. My evil heart was pleased for a second, and then a broken tooth dropped onto the tablecloth, followed instantly by a rather pendulous exclamation mark of drool. I managed to get her back to the house in something like one piece; she was still crying and cursing foreigners under the porch light.

My aunt is not exactly a collector, but, over the years, she had made some attempt at collecting the Dolls of the World, and she said there was no doubt she owned the best ones. The collection started when she and Uncle Fergus got married, with a clog dancer from Holland which still stood in a paper box covered in tulips, forty-five years after the honeymoon. The dolls were kept in a large, custom-built display cabinet fixed to the wall going up the stairs, and all the eyes seemed to follow you to the landing, each doll standing in silent testament to the trips Jessie and Fergus had made together. A Spanish flamenco dancer had sequins glued to her shoes and she brandished a black lace fan.

'What's this?' I said, stopping behind Aunt Jessie on the stairs to point through the glass cabinet.

'South African lady,' she said.

'That's a bit odd.'

'1976,' she said. 'Too hot. Rubbishy hotel, so far as I can remember. Not a very big pool. And that's the thing: your uncle Fergus liked a good swim. He only went abroad for the swimming.' For a second, the doll's periwinkle eyes stared right through me and somehow told me there was nothing more to say. Aunt Jessie climbed the last of the stairs, getting out of puff and still complaining about her tooth. 'Now I've hardly anything to chew with,' she said. 'I used to have a whole mouth. Nothing was any problem. Steaks, Highland Toffee, you name it.'

Aunt Jessie first saw Scotland on a visit to Culzean Castle with the typing pool from Farl & Leckie, a shirt-making firm in Kinsale. Jessie was quite high up in the company, Head of Sales in fact, but she liked to take outings with the office girls because the girls had more life about them. My uncle Fergus didn't have a great job then; he worked the gates at Culzean – I mean he took the tickets. Of course, Aunt Jessie thought that was a very glamorous thing to do with your life, to work in a castle filled with silver armour and paintings of the defeated English. In her best mode, she once told me the letters Fergus sent to her after that trip to Scotland were the sweetest things ever written by an idiot, and on receiving the third one she began making plans to leave County Cork, saying there were always jobs in the world for girls with brains and a clean driving licence. 'Scotland is just like Ireland,' she said. 'Full of songs nobody knows the words to. And piled up with dirty bottles.'

Since my own youth, I had liked to repeat the essentials of Jessie's story back to her, mainly because she was one of those people who seemed much grander and more rounded in retrospect. 'And you wanted for nothing once you were here,' I said, pulling down her bedroom blind to hide the rain and the memory of the Chinese. 'You wanted for nothing and lived in the first bungalow built in Kilmarnock.'

'You're just checking for Alzheimer's,' she said. 'It wasn't a bloody bungalow, it was a cottage. A proper cottage, with stairs. And it had been standing there since Robert Burns.'

She sat moaning on the edge of the bed, poking a finger into her mouth, and when I came down to the bathroom she yelled, 'You won't find any Tampax in there!' I laughed at that, and laughed again when I saw the bathroom was just as I remembered: not a room containing a medical cabinet, but a medical room, a health centre, a place where the world's most mysterious ailments might swiftly be remedied. There were pills for malaria and angina, though no one in the house had ever had that, creams for burns, ointments for bruises, blue guns and grey guns for whooping cough and asthma. The window was blocked off with boxes of Wind-Eze and cartons of Tums, and there were bottles of disinfectant dirty enough to require scrubbing with their own contents. Bandages, medical braces, and bindings of every sort covered the shelves, some of them still in their Boots bags. I found the oil of cloves on the corner of the bath; the bottle was undusty, the cap loose.

'Don't hurt me!' she said as I dabbed her gums. 'Some people just like to hurt other people. That's what they're like. Forever rubbing salt.'

'This is good stuff,' I said. 'You'll be ready for your dinner in ten minutes.'

Like an old woman in a Flemish painting, Jessie's face caught the light coming through the blind. Her eyes were as blue as those on the Dolls of the World, and she smiled in a manner quite obscure, before turning to the mirrored door. 'It wouldn't matter to me if I never ate a meal again,' she said.

I've always been rubbish with people feeling sorry for themselves, so I said nothing at first, then I met her eyes in the mirror and couldn't cope with that either.

'Did you put the sink in here?' I asked.

'Aye. That was me. I paid the man from Him'll Fix It to make a sink for your uncle Fergus, in case he wanted to wash his hands in the middle of the night. Save him going down the steps.'

'That was nice,' I said.

'He was such a clean-living man,' said Aunt Jessie.

Next to the bed, a rosewood chest gave support to a stuffed camel, a family mascot with lashes as long as an Egyptian summer. It reminded me of Polaroid days when each of us loved the notion of travel, when together we planned the great lives we might live, for weeks at a time, in the world called Abroad, waving from trains, making calls from hotels, learning bits of languages, and going our own way. Aunt Jessie was never one for the Spanish Steps or the foyers of old museums, but she loved those days of sea-water and tanning-oil stuck in the sand. It was never a break from life, but life itself. Aunt Jessie had done all that. She had gone from here. But the image she stared at every night – and now every day, as well as night – was her husband's one remaining oil, 'A Field Outside Dalry, 1913' by George Houston, a local painter who had loved Corot. The painting hung opposite the bed, and it seemed in itself to describe the difference between beauty experienced and beauty admired. It was basically a painting of a Scottish puddle, but it now meant the world to Aunt Jessie.

'Amanda. Amaryllis. Person of colour. Would you itch my poor feet?' she said.

'Lie down.'

'I'm not going to sleep,' she said. 'Once you start that. Once you start sleeping at three o'clock in the afternoon, that's you dead. I've seen it a hundred times. You start napping and you're dead in no time.'

I rubbed her feet, the tops of her socks. 'I'm quite the nurse today,' I said.

'Die Frau Ärztin!'

'I'm not German,' I said.

'No,' she said, 'but you love the Gerries. You're always reading those books. The brainboxes. Well, I'll tell you something for nothing: they weren't brainy enough to hold us back at Normandy.'

'Who's *us?*' I said. 'You and the English?'

'Don't start,' she said. 'The likes of you probably wishes the Gerries had won the war. Then you could speak German to one another all day and drive about in tanks.'

'Germany is not just about Nazis,' I said. 'There's more to Germany than that, thousands of years more.'

'I know,' she said. 'You don't have to tell me. I've seen *The Sound of Music.*'

Aunt Jessie took great pleasure in people's imperfections, and she was not frightened to admit it. 'If I was a contestant on *Mastermind*,' she said, 'I know what my specialist subject would be: "Your Mother's Failings: 1930–2002".' I wasn't going there, no way, so I just asked her to lean back on the pillows and say nothing for a while. 'Too much air isn't good for a fresh wound,' I said from the cupboard, promptly adopting her own style of medical wisdom. Through the door I knew she would be nodding in careful assent. 'Aye,' she said. 'That's right. I've often heard it said.'

My uncle's suits were mostly dark. Each had the scent of expired warmth, which is death to me, and pins on some lapels, The Rotary Club, The Bowling Club, The Burns Association, places where Fergus had gone in his retirement to take advantage of the cheap drink. He never lived in the world of designer labels, Paris and Milan, but of small Glasgow tailors who specialised in charcoal-coloured fabrics, men's handkerchiefs, and hats made to order, shops run by the kind of harassed people that my uncle assumed were the mainstay of Scottish life. Yet the smell of my uncle's suits spoke that afternoon of a life given over to equal measures of piety and mockery: a touch of candle wax, a hint of sherry.

Even before I found the letter, I began again to feel sorry for
Aunt Jessie. This was her life, and the cold suits were soon to
be taken from the house.

'Don't get lost in there,' she said.

'Have you a black bag, Aunt Jessie?'

'There's a roll of bags,' she said. 'Make sure there's no
coins in the pockets. Fergus was a helluva man for coins. If
you find any, we'll give them to the chapel. They've always
got a road for coins.'

Most suits were bagged by the time I found the letter. It
was stored in an inside pocket, folded twice, with a racing tip
– 'Pride of Orkney, 4.30 at Ayr' – scribbled on the other side.
The coat-hangers lightly touched one another on the rail,
their jingle the only thing to be heard apart from the sound
of Jessie's breathing. She was asleep.

> *I missed you at the car market. Come late*
> *tonight Randy O'Toole. I get upset not*
> *seeing you. There's a few tins of beer in the fridge.*

It was a wild notelet from a perfumed box, and reading it
made me think of school crushes, her name, 'May', scrawled
inside a briar of kisses. It had never occurred to me before
then how much I hated those Mays, those women who mess
about with men. They had no right to do that. I listened to
the cars passing on the road outside, and wondered how
many of the cars were driven by liars. It seemed right to wake
Jessie and show her the note; to let her finally put an end to
this man and his clean-living. I was almost decided: there was
dust on my hands, the powder of dead moths. My aunt had
every right to know that her husband Fergus had spent

nights drinking beer with women called May.

I tore up the letter and put the pieces into my purse. Going down the stairs I passed the eyes, but the light was gone and I couldn't see their colours any more. It gets strange in Ayrshire when the nights draw in; dark at four o'clock, our trees frozen in the public parks. Jessie's cat came to visit me as I sat in the living room waiting for the evening, the dark growing complex and the oil of cloves open on the table, ready for my aunt waking up with a feeling in her mouth. Mary the cat. She stepped past the carriage clock and leapt onto my knees when she saw a cloud of breath. I'd never known her to be so cold before, but I stroked her beautiful back and leaned down to place a kiss between her ears. 'Ben's gone back,' I whispered. 'He's gone home for good. What do you say to that, Mary?'

Nadya Radulova

Those Dead Birds on the Porch

Translated by Kalina Filipova

All those dead birds on the porch. When I opened up the house after being away for three months. It seems death hadn't left this place.

I left the suitcases in the hallway and methodically began to pull down the paper with which I had plastered all the windows. I took off the sheets that covered all the furniture, mirrors and pictures in the house. It was then that the smell hit me. The same smell from three months back, only perhaps that little bit stronger and more pervasive. Little whiffs of Lydol, Tramadol and morphine were still escaping from the vials and pill-boxes on the shelves; there were unused syringes in the drawers, unopened packets of Vilcacora, capsules of shark-liver oil and various other drugs that boost the immune system. I kept finding gauze, surgical scissors and methylated spirits in the most unexpected places. In my frantic efforts to get rid of everything as quickly as possible, I almost threw away the photo tacked to the kitchen cupboard, a photo of a much happier time.

I'm about four, in Granny's backyard and leafing through a picture book; sitting at the garden table beside me are my mother and father, playing cards. I have no idea who took the photo but they managed to capture the duck-yellow colour of my dress, the sun-bleached strands in my mother's hair, my father's delicate musician's fingers and his pleased smile of a winner. I remember it as clearly as if it were yesterday, that summer's day and the card game. All of a sudden my mother turns to me and asks: 'Would you like to have a little brother or sister?' Angry, almost in tears, I say no; that if that happened, I'd run away, far away from them; that I'd hate them. My parents calm me down and go back to their game. Neither the question nor the answer have entered the shot in any way. And in the next twenty-five years there is no one else in our family photos.

Even in high school I regretted my selfish outburst, which stopped my parents from having any more children. Much later, when they were ill and bed-ridden, I even blamed myself for having denied us all the chance of a bit more love and attention at such a hard time.

I dusted the photo carefully and put it back. Then I started on the floors and walls, and the cobwebs in high corners of the ceiling. It took me a whole day to rid the rooms of the smell and restore some of the colours. Late in the afternoon the bedroom looked bright and cheerful again with its Persian blue chest of drawers and the bedcovers with colourful pansies embroidered all over; even the faces in the photos seemed happier and kinder than before. Finally, I scraped the dry coffee caking the bottom of the coffee pot with such ferocity you'd think I was scraping away a painful memory; then I filled it with coffee and fresh water and turned on the hob.

Those past three months had done nothing to change anything in me, despite my huge efforts to run away from my recent past. Istanbul, Venice, Naples, then Tunisia and Morocco; and then the long return journey: Madrid, San Sebastian, Bilbao, Biarritz, Andorra and many, many more – places that left no trace except in dry travel notes, poor photographs and my unfortunate liver. Sex – whether because it was too casual and incidental, or because of the thin crust of ice which seemed to cover me from top to toe – fell far short of my expectations, except, perhaps, for that one night when I got high on pot on deck and then woke up in the cabin of that Slovenian couple, feeling all over that something wonderful had happened, even though I didn't have a clue what it might have been.

I think it was that night that I decided to stop running, to come back, collect all my stuff, find a buyer and take the first decisive step towards solving the problem of my past. By turning my back on it. In the home I grew up in. And now I was about to spend my first night in a house which was well disinfected and no longer belonged to anyone.

I had supper: bread and cheese, ham and half a bottle of Merlot. Then I watched a film and finished the wine. After midnight I started flipping channels frantically: old concerts I had seen or had on video; CNN and the BBC's three-day-old news; porn, which I wasn't in the mood for. I had a glass of whisky, turned off the TV and decided I would sleep on the couch in the living room. I went out like a light.

I was woken by the dog whining at my feet. I jumped up, only to realise that I hadn't had a dog for at least ten years now. I moved to the easy chair but I could still hear the whining. I began to doze off again. This time the sound came in straight through the window, flooding the quiet living room. My skin grew taught, my ears started buzzing, I could feel my veins turning phosphorescent in the dark. The sound was that of someone weeping feebly, meekly. I went up to the window and looked out. There seemed to be some sort of white snowdrift right next to the bed of lily-of-the-valley. It moved almost imperceptibly. Numb with fear, I opened the door and found myself staring at the vague outlines of a body. It was a girl, eighteen or nineteen, her calf-length dress stained and torn, her knees and elbows sticking out; she was all skin and bones. At first I thought she must be a young vagrant who'd sneaked in to find some shelter. But how could she have sneaked in: the only way out into the garden was through the house . . .

The girl looked up at me and started sobbing more loudly. I bent down to lift her. She was very light: as though there was something missing in her, something lacking – organs, bones, fluids, a past . . . Lately, light bodies seemed to me particularly sinister. I carried her into the room and put her in one of the chairs. Her head lolled sideways.

'Who are you? How did you come in? Did anyone hurt you?'

The girl went on sobbing.

'Ida. My name is Ida,' she managed to say. 'I'm on my own.'

'Have you run away from home? Have your parents hurt you?'

'I got thrown out. I was caught stealing and . . .'

She couldn't have had a normal home. She looked under-nourished, there was a sour smell coming from her, she hadn't changed in days. I decided not to ask any more questions. Instead, I gave her a clean towel and took her to the bathroom. Ida just stood there, though: she was too weak to take off her dress. I helped her. She had nothing on underneath but her panties. Her breasts were almost boyish: I doubt she'd ever worn a bra. I pushed her gently under the shower and turned on the hot water. When I began to lather her, her hands started trembling uncontrollably. A minute later she was trembling all over and it was all I could do to keep her from collapsing onto the tiles. I couldn't hug her: I felt pity for her but also disgust.

I took Ida back into the living room and settled her into the easy chair. I put down a mug of tea and some sandwiches, and biscuits beside her. She ate up everything within a couple of minutes, then rushed to the bathroom and vomited. When, pale and trembling, she came back into the room and sank down into the easy chair, I could no longer contain myself and asked: 'How did you get into the garden?'

'I just climbed over the wall; I had to hide.'

What kind of superhuman strength did this scrawny child possess, to be able to climb over a six-foot wall?

'What did you steal?'

'Things – coffee and cigarettes from the supermarket, alcohol, nice underwear sometimes, jewellery.'

'Who makes you do that?'

'No one. I sell the stuff. I want to get away.'

'From your parents? From home?'

Ida burst into tears again and I decided I shouldn't ask any more questions. I took out what clothes and underwear I had left from my high-school years, dressed her in them and put her to bed on the sofa.

I went into the bedroom and, just to be on the safe side, shut firmly the door to the living room.

*　*　*

The next three days I hardly left the house. I would only go out early in the morning to buy fresh bread and vegetables and a newspaper: every day I expected a note to appear in the 'Missing Persons' section announcing a girl had gone missing and was wanted by the police. Then I would bolt the front door and go on cleaning the rooms and cooking meals for Ida. The little thief hardly spoke to me. She did mention, though, and several times, that she wouldn't be bothering me for much longer. She said she'd managed to bring some of her money along and was planning to go to the seaside where she hoped no one would recognise her and she'd find a job more easily. I wondered where she could have hidden the money, having come in that tattered dress and without any luggage. It turned out she'd left it with a high-school friend who'd keep it for her until Ida rang her.

'Aren't you afraid your family or the police might knock on the door any minute? What should I tell them? I can't hide you here forever . . .'

'I ran for a long time before I got here. They won't find me.'

'Don't you miss your parents?'

'I don't have any parents,' Ida said calmly.

I could see her regaining her strength by the hour. Gradually a brave, confident body took shape inside those old school clothes of mine; the colour returned to her cheeks, her lips became full and beautiful, her ankles grew strong and her knees stopped trembling. I kept plying her with food and vitamins. I gave her milk and broccoli, carrots, spinach, and buckwheat. I made her eat nuts and poured her a glass of red wine every evening. The rest of the bottle I would finish on my own, in my bedroom. On the third day

Ida offered to help me with the cleaning and packing. Gradually, she became completely absorbed in her work. She would handle the silverware with a devotion that revealed respect for a past she didn't share. She carefully packed away the photographs, asking me about the people in them, trying to memorise who they were. I could hear her softly repeating their names later as though she was trying to file them away in her memory so that she'd be able to return to them when necessary. She polished the glasses before wrapping them up in paper and arranging them in boxes – glasses she would never drink from. She sorted my father's notebooks by date, sticking little pieces of paper in their upper left-hand corner. I was grateful to her because I still found it difficult to enter into and explore the world which, three months ago, had abandoned me so painfully.

'Why don't you let me live here for a while after you leave? It's not very likely you'll find a buyer that quickly. I'll pay you rent,' Ida said, taping another cardboard box closed.

'I'm hoping I will find a buyer quickly . . . But, of course, you can stay until it's sold. You don't need to pay anything. I'm just worried someone will recognise you and then we'll both be in trouble.'

'They won't. I mean, you didn't, did you? Why should the neighbours? And anyway, I'll make sure I don't go out much.'

I couldn't say no. She seemed so badly hurt, I just couldn't find it in me to turn her out.

That evening I had rather more to drink than usual. Ida was still very quiet but seemed absorbed in my stories and kept wanting more. I went on and on – about my travels, the

ships, the men I'd met. I would often burst out laughing at
the memories of all my silly flirting and the empty mornings
after a night of shabby, uninspiring sex.

'Perhaps you shouldn't drink every night . . .' Ida said and
there was concern in her eyes. 'How long have you been like
that?'

'And how long have you been going around supermarkets,
stealing?!' I snapped back at her.

'Sorry. I didn't mean to offend. But you're so pretty. And
clever. You should take better care of yourself. But – I do
apologise . . .'

'I've been drinking since I lost them. I can't sleep otherwise.'

'I can't sleep much either. Not for years now. And I don't
even know whom I might have lost, or when.'

I felt bad about snapping at her: she couldn't have had it
easier than me. For the first time I felt the need to touch her.
I stretched my hand and gently caressed the inside of her
hand. She smiled and blushed slightly.

It was well past midnight when I turned out the light in the
living room and wished Ida good night. This time I couldn't
bring myself to shut the bedroom door behind me.

It wasn't long before she came. I was still awake and heard
her soft barefoot steps across the wooden floor.

'May I sleep in your bed?'

'Yes, child.'

I lifted the blanket and Ida crept in beside me. There was
hardly any trace left of my former disgust. Now she seemed
cleaner and stronger than me. Her arms and her legs were
supple and warm. Her belly, pressed against mine, no longer

repelled me. Her skin glowed as if it had been rubbed with lemon peel and milk. Her hair smelled of pine, and this was not due to the expensive shampoos in my bathroom. I was surprised and moved, despite myself, and soon I could feel my whole body vibrating. Ida seemed to become aware of this: she looked up in the dark and then she lowered her lips towards my breasts. She began to kiss them and there was nothing shy or inexperienced about it: she kissed them as I would have kissed hers. Without even asking her. Without expecting her to answer.

I felt dizzy with wine and excitement. I closed my eyes for an instant.

I dreamt I was riding my first bicycle in our backyard.

It's small and red, and it's actually a tricycle. Our backyard isn't very big, so I go round and round in circles by the walls. Tall white walls. I'm peddling harder and harder. A fine paste of white plaster and green ivy looms before my eyes. Any moment now I'll fly off my bike but then suddenly I see something strange and indistinct on the porch. My mother, my father and – something else. A child. It looks like me and has a shiny new red bicycle, just like mine. Is that me? But how could it be: I'm over here? And if it isn't me, then who is that other girl? I can feel the horror rising in my throat, I let go of the handlebars and smash into the white-and-green paste . . .

I wake up drenched in sweat. I'm feeling sick. I try to keep my head still, as though it's a bowl of the last soup I'm ever going to have in my life, and I shouldn't spill a single drop. Ida is sleeping quietly beside me. I somehow have to reach the toilet. Swaying, I manage to get through the door into the living room and then into the bathroom. I sit on the toilet and pee in the dark. I splash some cold water on my face. Then touch my lips to the faucet and drink thirstily, letting the water run down my face and neck and between my breasts.

I go back through the living room. The alcohol seems to have sharpened my senses because once again I can smell the odour of various medicines in the air. I can even tell their different dosage by the smell. The strongest ones are taught like bowstrings and when they snap, they directly pierce my nose. A wave of nausea comes over me and I have to lean against the wall so I don't collapse. There are empty white squares in white frames where the photos used to hang. One of them is very, very large. We've never had such a large photo in the house. Then it turns out that's my bedroom door. Why don't I remember closing it? I tiptoe inside and head for the bed. Ida is still fast asleep. She looks so tiny. As though she has shrunk terribly in her sleep. I want to look at her for a while before I go back to bed. Standing above her, I lift the cover. Suddenly it all comes to me in a flash. And I recognise her. That child's body framed by the white of the sheets. A tiny three or four year old. And she looks just like me, as though she's come straight out of one of my child-hood photos. Or as if she's only just entered one. Except she's slightly fairer, slightly smaller. She's wearing the same duck-yellow dress. The one I wore that afternoon twenty-five years ago. I don't know who took the photo but he seems to have missed something extremely important. And now it's too late to rewind the film – and let that other one enter the shot.

193

I reached over, grabbed my pillow, and pressed it down as hard as I could over the poor sleeping child's face; I pressed and pressed until my wrists started turning blue.

About the Authors

J. Robert Lennon is the author of five books, including *Mailman* and *Pieces for the Left Hand*. He lives in upstate New York.

David Almond grew up in a large Catholic family on Tyneside. His first novel for children, *Skellig*, won the Carnegie Medal and the Whitbread Award, and became an international bestseller. The novels, plays and stories that followed have brought popular success, widespread critical acclaim and a string of major prizes. His work is translated into over twenty languages, and has been adapted for film, radio and stage. 'Slog's Dad' is from an ongoing sequence, *Stories from the Middle of the World?*, set in Felling on Tyne. The first book-length collection of these stories, *Counting Stars*, is published by Hodder. He lives with his family in Northumberland. His most recent novel is *Clay*.

Natalia Smirnova was born in 1962 in the Siberian city of Yakutsk and later moved to Yekaterinburg in the Urals. A philologist by training, she taught at the Urals University before moving to Moscow to work for a publishing house. Smirnova has received wide acclaim for her collections of short stories and novels, which include *Businesswoman* and *The Clever and the Impudent*. Her story 'The Women and the Shoemakers' won the Fellowship of the Hawthornden

International Writers' Retreat award. Her work has been translated into Italian, French and English.

Margaret Wilkinson is a playwright and short-story writer. Recipient of an Arts Council Award to travel to Russia, Ukraine and the USA to research Anton Chekhov and Raymond Carver, she wrote a play, *Kaput!*, weaving together their short stories. Her latest radio play, *Passover*, was recently broadcast on BBC Radio 4 Woman's Hour. Passionate about the short story, she was one of the creators of the campaign to Save Our Short Story. She teaches prose and scriptwriting on the MA in Creative Writing course at the University of Newcastle upon Tyne.

Georgi Gospodinov is one of the most well-known Bulgarian writers. His first two books of poetry were received enthusiastically by readers and critics in Bulgaria and won national literary prizes. He is co-author of two books of literary mystification. His debut novel, *Natural Novel*, was a bestseller in Bulgaria and has been widely translated and reviewed. He has also written *And Other Stories*, a collection of short stories, and a play called *D.J.* (an abbreviation of Don Juan), which won the 2004 National Award for the Best Dramatic Text of the Year. His poetry was included in the English-language anthology *A Fine Line: New Poetry from Eastern and Central Europe* (Arc 2004). Georgi Gospodinov works as editor for the *Literary Newspaper* (a literary and cultural weekly) and has a PhD from the Institute of Literature at the Bulgarian Academy of Sciences.

Ali Smith was born in Inverness in 1962 and lives in Cambridge. Her latest collection of short stories is *The Whole Story and Other Stories* (Penguin 2004) and her latest novel is *The Accidental* (Hamish Hamilton 2005).

David Means' most recent collection of stories is *The Secret Goldfish*, published by 4th Estate. His stories have appeared in the *New Yorker, Harper's Magazine, Esquire* and numerous other publications. His previous book, *Assorted Fire Events*, won the *Los Angeles Times* Book Prize and was a finalist for the National Book Critics Circle Award. Born and raised in Michigan, he now lives in Nyack, New York, with his wife and twins.

Evgeny Popov was born in 1946 in Krasnoyarsk, Siberia, moved to Moscow in the 1960s and later graduated from the Moscow Institute of Geology. He then spent many years travelling the width and breadth of Russia. His involvement with the illegal publication of the uncensored literary almanac *Metropol* in 1981 resulted in his immediate expulsion from the Writers' Union. A long period in literary exile followed until the late 1980s when, under the new conditions of political freedom, he was widely published both at home and abroad. He has written more than two hundred stories and five novels, including *The Soul of the Patriot* and *The Merry-Making in Old Russia*, published in twenty countries.

Courttia Newland is the author of the critically acclaimed novels *The Scholar, Society Within* and *Snakeskin*. He has contributed to the anthologies *Disco 2000, New Writers 8, Afrobeat, The Time Out Book of London Short-Stories,*

England Calling and *Tell Tales Vol 2*. He is the editor of an anthology of new black writing in Britain, *IC3*, and of *Tell Tales Vol 1*. His novella, *A Dying Wish*, will be published by Abacus in Autumn 2006. A short-story collection, *Music for the Off Key*, is published by Peepal Tree Press.

Andrew Crumey lives in Newcastle upon Tyne and is the author of five novels, including *Mobius Dick* and *Mr Mee*, which won the Scottish Arts Council Book Award and was long-listed for the Man Booker Prize. He has a PhD in theoretical physics and is currently literary editor of *Scotland On Sunday*.

Julia Darling lost her fight with cancer in April 2005. She was a novelist, poet and playwright. Her published work includes: a collection of short stories, *Bloodlines* (Panurge); two novels, *Crocodile Soup* and *The Taxi Driver's Daughter* (Penguin); and two collections of poetry, *Sudden Collapses in Public Places* and *Apology for Absence* (Arc Press). With Cynthia Fuller, Julia edited *The Poetry Cure* (Bloodaxe), a collection of poetry about health. Her work for theatre and radio was collected in *Eating the Elephant and Other Plays* (New Writing North). She was awarded a £60,000 Northern Rock Foundation Writer's Award in 2003, and was a fellow at the School of English Language and Linguistics at the University of Newcastle upon Tyne. More information about Julia's life and work can be found at www.juliadarling.co.uk

Rajeev Balasubramanyam's first novel, *In Beautiful Disguises* (Bloomsbury 2000), was the winner of a Betty Trask Prize and long-listed for the Guardian First Fiction

Prize. He is working on his second novel, *The Dreamer*, based on a short story which won an Ian St James Prize in 2001. He was the recent winner of the Clarissa Luard Award and an Arts Council Writers' Award and has published short stories in various anthologies, including *New Writing 12*. He lives in Manchester.

Andrew O'Hagan was born in Glasgow in 1968. In 1995 he wrote *The Missing* and in 1999 he published his first novel, *Our Fathers*, which was short-listed for the Man Booker Prize, the Whitbread First Novel Award, the International IMPAC Dublin Literary Award, the John Llewellyn Rhys Prize, and was winner of the Holtby Prize for Fiction. His latest novel, *Personality*, was published in 2003. He won the E. M. Forster Award from the American Academy of Arts and Letters, and was named one of Granta's Best of Young British Novelists. *Personality* also won the James Tait Black Memorial Prize for Fiction. Andrew O'Hagan's work is published in the London Review of Books and the New Yorker. Since 2000, he has been a Unicef Ambassador.

Nadya Radulova was born in 1975 and graduated from the Faculty of Slavic Studies, Sofia University, in 1999. In 2001 she acquired her MPhil degree from Central European University, Budapest, and the Open University. Her academic interests are related to the field of Comparative Literature, Gender Studies and literary translation. Radulova also works as an editor of the monthly journal for gender, language and culture, *Altera*, and as a translator of poetry and fiction. She is author of three poetry books: *Tongue-tied*

Name (1996), *Albas* (2000) and *Cotton, Glass and Electricity* (2004). Her work has been translated into English, Russian, Czech and Turkish.

New Writing North

New Writing North is the writing development agency for the north-east of England. We are a unique organisation within the UK, merging as we do individual development work with writers across all media with educational work and the production of creative projects. We work with writers from different genres and forms to develop career opportunities, new commissions, projects, residencies, publications and live events.

We manage the Northern Writers' Awards and the Northern Rock Foundation Writer's Award (currently the largest literary award in the UK and worth £60,000 to the winning writer) and support writers at all stages of their careers by mentoring and by the creation of professional-development training initiatives and mentoring.

We work in partnership with writers, theatres and producers to develop new writing for the stage and have initiated work and new commissions with many of the theatre companies in our region. We also produce new plays as part of a regional touring consortium.

Through our international work we aspire to create partnerships and projects for writers from our region with international counterparts. We are currently developing projects with partners in Bulgaria, Siberia and the Czech Republic. In autumn 2006 we will be working with Glas publishers in Moscow to produce a new collection of short stories, *War & Peace*, by Russian writers; the book will be launched in the UK with a national tour to festivals and venues.

New Writing North has published a number of books including: *Bound*, a collection of short stories which takes the form of an artist's book by sculptor Tanya Axford; the stage play of *Kaput!* by Margaret Wilkinson which was performed as part of the Festival of Stories in 2004; *Eating the Elephant and Other Plays* by Julia Darling; and *Magnetic North*, an anthology of new work from North-East writers.

For more information on our work:
www.newwritingnorth.com
www.nr-foundationwriters.com
www.wordmavericks.com
www.acknowledgedland.com

For more information on the short story in the UK:
www.theshortstory.org.uk

Acknowledgements

The editors would like to thank the following people and organizations: Arts Council England, North East; Duska Radosavljevic; Natasha Perova at Glas in Moscow; Kate Griffin (Arts Council England); Northern Stage; Live Theatre; British Council (UK, Russia and Bulgaria); Flambard Press; University of Newcastle School of English.

The Festival of Stories project received financial support from the following partners: Northern Rock Foundation; Esmee Fairbairn Foundation; Arts Council England; Newcastle City Council.

New Writing North would like to acknowledge the support of the Cultural Sector Development Initiative run by Arts Council England, North East. We also acknowledge support from the European Regional Development Fund of the European Union.